«major writers»

FLANAGAN
FOX
MATTHEWS
O'CONNOR

BEST OHIO FICTION

YOUNGER OHIO FICTION WRITERS

feil
flanagan
o'connor
schildhouse

Edited and Introduced
by Larry Smith & Laura Smith

bottom dog press

Copyright © Bottom Dog Press 1987

ISBN 0-933087-10-1

Cover Designed by Zita Sodeika
Palacio type set at BookMasters

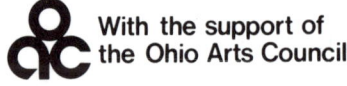 With the support of
the Ohio Arts Council

Published by Bottom Dog Press Inc.
c/o Firelands College, Huron, Ohio

CONTENTS

INTRODUCTION
by Larry Smith & Laura Smith

YOUNGER OHIO FICTION WRITERS

BRIAN FEIL
Fitzweiler's Gone
9

ANNE FLANAGAN
Family Portrait
26

JOHN O'CONNOR
Callaban's Lieutenants
34

AMY SCHILDHOUSE
Alysa's Father
46

MAJOR OHIO FICTION WRITERS

ROBERT FLANAGAN
All Alone and Blue
52

ROBERT FOX
Frito and the Strong Man
79

JACK MATTHEWS
The Smoke of Invisible Fires
102

PHILIP F. O'CONNOR
The Voice of the Bird
129

INTRODUCTION

The time is right for BEST OHIO FICTION, a collection of eight stories by some of Ohio's best fiction writers. Not only is the art of fiction writing and reading alive in Ohio, nationwide we are experiencing a fiction renaissance. We've moved nicely from a droll questioning of "Is the novel dead?" to an exciting "Who are you reading?" as more people are choosing to enrich their lives through the creative dance between the writer—the work—the reader.

It's a storied world we live in after all, whether we read those stories in the news or in the bathroom, whether we tell them around the kitchen table, to our children at night, or to ourselves as we drive. Today we can find good (and bad) fiction in almost any magazine (REDBOOK to READER'S DIGEST to ROLLING STONE to RIVERWIND), and in our neighborhood bookstores as well as our drug and grocery stores. We are constantly told stories through film and television to help us escape or to make new sense of our lives. The effect of the new technology—video and audio tapes—seems to have been more one of arousal than somnolence. Perhaps the need to enlarge our lives through the imagination has simply grown through all the non-answers technology has provided.

Good fiction is a part of the high-touch resolution we need in our lives, and its vitality is in itself a hopeful sign. For, as Flannery O'Connor put so well, "People without hope not only don't write novels, but what is more to the point, they don't read them." Contemporary fiction is both a question and an affirmation, essentially a search in a time of crisis that often leads to a discovery. In answer to our need to know the story of life, fiction reveals a mythic world in which past, present, and future are unified and undifferentiated. When we allow ourselves into the world of fiction we come to know life beyond history in a present that is as endless as our search.

Though BEST OHIO FICTION draws on writers born or living in Ohio, they and their fiction are not confined by it. Certainly each state could and should produce a similar collection—these are our best. And yet, there has always been a centrality about Ohio and its shared Ohioness, a mythic Midwest that engenders while it instills a sense of place at once particular and universal. Life may not be any simpler here, than along our East and West Coast, but it is more located, within the American grain—"the heart of it all" as we say in Ohio. And, though many native Ohio writers move elsewhere to live and work, what they carry with them is a full and sharp sense of place garnered from their Ohio youth. Ohio has produced writers just as it has presidents.

What characterizes the atmosphere for fiction writing in Ohio is its variety and its fecudnity. There exists a strong modern tradition of Ohio story tellers who have used the Ohio setting to reveal life here and beyond—best typified by Sherwood Anderson, but also by such diverse voices as William Dean Howells, Zane Grey, James Thurber, Ambrose Bierce, and for a time O. Henry. Writers who have successfully taken that tradition of realism and humor into the complexity of contemporary life and art include such talents as Thomas Berger, James Purdy, Toni Morrison, Herbert Gold, Don Robertson, David Wagoner, Daniel Keyes, John Jakes, Hollis Summers, and of course Helen Hoover Santmyer. Our four major writers assembled here belong to that list: Jack Matthews, Philip F. O'Connor, Robert Flanagan, and Robert Fox.

What characterizes the work of these contemporaries is a poetic realism (most of them are also poets), a sense of humor as well as place, a fine ear for dialogue and dialect, and a mythic sense of life in the Midwest, proving that the imagination may actually be sharpened by the sameness of the Midwestern landscape.

Another witness to the vitality of fiction in Ohio can be seen in the activities of the creative writing programs at our state universities and private colleges. Matthews (Ohio University), O'Connor (Bowling Green State University), Flanagan (Ohio Wesleyan), and Fox (Ohio University and the Ohio Arts Council's Writers-in-the Schools Program) are all teachers of creative writing, serving the role as elders in the craft, and they have all helped some remarkable students. Additionally there are numerous writers groups and conferences providing a necessary expectation and support for Ohio's developing and working writers.

To bring this work to its audience there is the active body of literary small and university presses and magazines publishing the best fiction from and beyond Ohio. Though Ohio lacks a large fiction publisher (no guarantee of quality anyway), there are such book publishers as Ohio University and Ohio State University Presses and some vital small presses like Carpenter, Bottom Dog, and Cumberland Press offering thoughtful and dynamic alternatives to corporate publishing. Some of the magazines publishing fiction would include the major established reviews such as : KENYON, ANTIOCH, THE OHIO REVIEW, THE OHIO JOURNAL, GAMUT, MID-AMERICAN REVIEW; as well as a lively and colorful network of smaller magazines: RIVERWIND, THE PLOUGH, PIG IRON, THE NEW KENT QUARTERLY, OHIO RENAISSANCE REVIEW, GREEN FEATHERS, MARK, GAMBIT, LIAR'S CORNER ALMANAC, BLACK RIVER REVIEW, etc.

Most importantly, there is a large and diverse body of independent writers out there turning real life into a very real fiction.

The art of fiction is alive in Ohio.

* * *

BEST OHIO FICTION is divided neatly into two sections: First, our four major writers and the stories they share. We have placed their work together in the second half and provided a photo and a critical, biographical sketch for each. Thus, their generosity, persistence, and achievement are represented here. They have each produced a strong body of fiction, worked to develop the art of fiction in this state and elsewhere, and received national recognition for their achievement. Their original unpublished stories testify to all of the above. They also have served as our final judges in selecting the four Younger Ohio Fiction Writers and provided detailed comments on the work of the nine top stories. We are all indebted to them for their good work.

Secondly, we are proud to feature the four winners of the Younger Ohio Fiction Writers Contest sponsored by Bottom Dog Press. The fifty stories entered (a sign of vitality in itself) were first of all screened by our editors who determined the best nine stories—five of whom receive honorable mention here:

HONORABLE MENTIONS: Ann Hinkle "Reunions," M. A. Neff "Putting Torey to Bed," Edward L. Beardshear "Talk," John Druska "The Bathers," and Jack Smith "Grey Dawn."

The stories were then submitted anonymously and independently to our panel of four judges—Flanagan, Fox, Matthews, and O'Connor—who scored and commented on each entry. These scores were then tabulated (the comments passed on to the writers) and the four best stories determined: Brian Feil—"Fitzweiler's Gone," Anne Flanagan—"Family Portrait," John O'Connor—"Calaban's Lieutenants," and Amy Schildhouse—"Alysa's Father." All winning selections received high scores by at least five of our six judges. [I suppose we should comment on our surprise that two of our winners turned out to be the son and daughter of two of our major writers. The coincidence is striking, but once we read the stories or once you read them there is no surprise as to why they were selected.] The excellence of all four stories is sign of a vital future for Ohio fiction.

. . . Larry Smith

* * *

Here are our four Younger Ohio Fiction Writers who present the opening act for our drama of fiction here.

Brian Feil grew up in Findlay, Ohio, and has held a variety of jobs across the country: lumberjack, clamdigger, flag pole painter and Fotomat cashier. He graduated from Bowling Green State University and Case Western Reserve University.

"Fitzweiler's Gone," Feil's first published story, places troop 303 in a situation that turns the cocky boy scouts into confused and frightened kids. Filling the gap left by their leader and good scout Fitzweiler is Roy "Sarge" Bevens, a Vietnam War veteran who catches the troop of adolescents in his own inner conflict.

Robert Fox calls "Fitzweiler's Gone" a "story of initiation told in a new and fresh way . . . The author takes a great risk and succeeds." Phil O'Connor agrees calling it "an exciting story front to back with a good rendition of characters and fine exploitation of a strong story line." Jack Matthews calls it "a good ambitious story."

Anne Flanagan, born in 1965 in Chicago, is a graduate of Ohio Wesleyan who majored in theater and journalism. She also acted in several college productions and twice won the Ohio Wesleyan F. C. Hunt Creative Writing Award. She has worked as a T.V. and radio news reporter and as an editorial assistant for Mack-Taylor Film Production in New York City.

Flanagan's "Family Portrait" is a descriptive account of Christmas dinner at Grandma's house in Toledo. The Cutters, a family separated by divorce and college, attempt to revive attachments that have weakened from disuse. It is a complex arrangement that leads to a tense but comical dinner and a competitive traditional game of charades. The situations and tensions are realistic, like peering through a window at a real family reunion.

"Comical and complex. A large cast of characters deftly handled," writes Robert Flanagan of "Family Portrait" and adds "Under the comedy is a blues note."

John O'Connor was born in Potsdam, New York, in 1963. He is a graduate of St. Lawrence University and is completing an MFA degree in creative writing at Bowling Green State University where he received a Devine Fellowship for Best Fiction Manuscript. His stories have appeared in BIG TWO-HEARTED RIVER and PHOEBE: THE GEORGE MASON REVIEW. He has been active in theater as an actor and director and has been assistant editor to MID-AMERICAN REVIEW. O'Connor also teaches and coaches wrestling.

Told from within the life of marines, John O'Connor's "Callaban's Lieutenants" is a description of the mentality of America's "fighting men" as they learn to face today's enemy with all its evils.

Phil O'Connor calls this story most original and states, "Its sense of character and situation impresses." Robert Fox writes, "I usually don't like army stories, but this has enough new in it to succeed."

Amy Schildhouse is a freelance writer of fiction, poetry and non-fiction. She lives in Columbus and has published stories in OHIO JEWISH CHRONICLE and AMERICAN STORIES (Green Street Press).

INTRODUCTION

Schildhouse's story "Alysa's Father" is a look at the subtle, sobering effect of reality on boyhood admiration. It is narrated from the backseat of the car by 13 year old David whose admiration lies with Mr. Schulman. From his leather boots to the smell of his cologne, Mr. Schulman is all a father and a man should be in the boy's eyes.

Robert Flanagan describes "Alysa's Father" as, "A fast-paced story with accuracy of narrative voice." Without saying too much Schildhouse succeeds in being "Very true to character and emotion," continues Flanagan.

All four of these new authors possess a fresh literary talent and spirit that is apparent in their stories. They embody the truth that Ohio still nurtures a creative spirit.

. . . Laura Smith

YOUNGER
OHIO FICTION WRITERS

BRIAN FEIL

FITZWEILER'S GONE

Fitzweiler was gone, retired these three weeks as scoutmaster and off to the Methodist Retirement Home up north with his wife Flora. It had been a disorienting three weeks for the boys he left behind, but especially so for Eric, who found great stability in the old scoutmaster.

So Eric had to settle for memory in lieu of flesh and blood. Little by little he wore Fitzweiler away until a workable image emerged. Fitzweiler: glorious in khaki, magnificent belly, wonderfully blousy riding breeches (though he forewent the ordeal of buttoning the top button), rainbow decorations, perfectly Flora-ironed kerchief, knee socks with red tassels on top, and (of course) the ranger hat given him in 1946 by Omar Bradley when he left the General's staff. That was Fitzweiler. He was as close as a human being could get to looking like Elmer Fudd and still claim this planet as home. Yet in a world of incoming missiles, he was a single impenetrable slab of granite, the patriarch of Troop 303, the Great White Father of the roaring campfire.

When Eric's footing became shaky and the ground rumbled, there was Fitzweiler, slightly bent forward, ranger hat set perfectly parallel to the ground, resplendent in khaki knee socks and red tassels. So strong an image Fitzweiler left, Eric wondered if he hadn't committed the scoutmaster to memory long before his departure. But this Fitzweiler developed no squeaky voice or skin conditions or hair growths in weird places or the necessity of an athletic supporter in gym class. At least for the moment, it didn't matter if Fitzweiler was here or not, or if Troop 303 had no scoutmaster.

But the boys met every Tuesday night anyhow. Derek Hart presided, picked a topic for each night, and then watched the meeting quickly deteriorate. In the corner, Neal and Rick played their favorite game:

"Hooters."
"Uh . . . mogambas."
"Milk funds."
"Headlights."
"Um, um, ummm . . . uhhhh."
"You lose!"
"No, no . . . cawockas!"
"What?"
"Cawockas."
"Oh, come on!"
"Really, cawockas!"

Why did it seem to Eric that every meeting unwound the same way? And why did everyone say the same words every Tuesday night? He couldn't escape the feeling that he had something to do with it all, that he was responsible for this sameness.

Derek: Okay, guys. Okay. Okay, guys. Okay. Okay, guys? Guys? Guy-uys?! Okay?

Steve: Man. I could go for a cigarette right now. Anybody got one? Man. I need one now. You got one? Jesus.

Derek: Come on, we're in a church, you know.

Steve: Don't sweat it, don't sweat it. I'll take responsibility. Don't sweat it.

Eric sat and listened, feeling sorry for Derek letting control slip away again, and somehow liking Steve—though that would surprise most in the troop. Eric was thought to be a straight arrow, sitting quietly up front in the corner, never talking unless asked a question and then answering in a very, very low voice and in as few words as possible. Every election they tried to draft him, but he would have no part of it—not even Quartermaster or Chaplain. He had comfortably removed himself from such proceedings. Besides, Eric was far too cynical. He was basically and profoundly distrustful of the trappings of age and that certainly included any office holdings.

Steve, on the other hand, embraced all trappings, and simultaneously. He lived a decade ahead of the rest and himself. The first to smoke, the first to drink (although no one had ever seen him): Steve was a man among boys. And he flaunted his adultness with every new vice—or so it seemed to Eric. But Eric liked Steve despite the pretentiousness or maybe because Steve lived so defiantly in the disgust and grunginess of adultdom.

Steve was openly and brashly (but not scornfully) cynical: the acknowledged rebel of Troop 303. Once, when Fitzweiler found a cigar on Steve, he sent him to Reverend Blake, who sat talking quietly to the boy for nearly an hour in the rectory in a whisper so low that Steve had to lean in close to the minister to hear. Reverence Blake's breath smelled like wintergreen—not of the stale pink lozenges, but of the real stuff that Fitzweiler used to hunt for under the brierbushes. Steve recognized goodness, could smell it on the Reverend's breath, could see it in Fitzweiler's straightness. But Fitzweiler was gone now and Steve could recognize evil just as well.

Eric was no outlaw. And he wasn't so sure he had the power of recognition. Eric was too busy trying to control what he saw and heard and tasted, trying to order, plug it all in as he had with Fitzweiler. But the categories themselves kept changing and just lately it seemed. Not "good" or "evil"—they wouldn't do. Too many things had slipped from one to the other in the last couple years. Maybe "stable" and "unstable." But those were unstable words themselves. Eric judged and tossed what he saw in one pile or the other (though the heaps remained nameless). That was his cynicism: the cynicism of A or B. And his cynicism was stored (no, enshrined) in a small private room. Eric watched from the room, quietly looking out a solitary circular window, out over a walled-in garden, dreaming and scoffing alternately. Steve's was the cynicism of excess. He ran around and around the outside, shouting out of breath, carelessly throwing what he saw on the front porch and in the shrubbery for all the neighbors to see. That was really the only difference.

"Hey, doughbutt! Watcha hiding in there?" Steve snapped Woody in the rear with his kerchief.

"You're so stupid, you're dumb," Woody said over his shoulder.

"Brilliant! Give me a pencil so I can write that down, willya?" The Tenderfoots laughed, half-afraid of Steve, half-inebriated by the idea of a roomful of boys with no adult.

Footsteps sounded in the hall and Reverend Blake entered the Grotto. Derek's hand went up, using his power as Senior Patrol Leader to exercise the first rule of scouting ("When the hand goes up, the mouth goes shut"). Reverend Blake stood a second longer in the doorway, waiting for the closest thing to silence, and the boys noticed for the first time there was someone with him. The someone lingered in the hallway and finally sneaked in behind Reverend Blake as if unsure of any room called the Grotto (though it was only an unused room in the corner of the church basement, renamed to satisfy the bold and lusty needs of scouting). He stood behind and off to the side as the minister talked, looking nowhere in particular, but seeming uncomfortable, like he was always conscious of the ceiling. Reverend Blake talked about how the trustees had searched many weeks for the perfect scoutmaster; how they thought they had found the right man; how he was sure the boys would agree.

And then Reverend Blake left. The new scoutmaster looked relieved, as though the ceiling had been raised an inch, but not completely removed. His name was Roy Bevens. And, according to Derek (whose father was chairman of the trustees) this is who Roy Bevens was:

—Joined church six months ago
—Married
—Wife member all her life
—Regular attendance
—New baby
—Recently promoted to supervisor in his accounting section
—Ex-army sergeant
—Veteran

That was Roy Bevens. It could have been any one of the boys' fathers twenty or more years ago, but it wasn't. It was Roy Bevens. He wore a suit, probably the one he wore to work that day, looking like it was fresh from the rack with the hanger still in it. It's not that it doesn't fit, Eric thought, he just doesn't fit it. He was Marvel Comics fleshed out: there was nothing rounded off about him. That was why the suit wasn't right. Roy was all right angles and parallel lines. If there was ever a granite image, Roy was it. And Eric did not even have to remember—the 6-foot 2-inch slab loomed in front of him.

Roy stood and looked at them, up and down the rows on both sides of the room, not like a judge but more like a dentist as if faced with a fresh mouth ready for extraction. Painless Roy Bevens. And then he broke a smile, and everyone gathered a cumulative sigh and smiled, too.

Eric also smiled, though he thought of Fitzweiler and looked at Roy Bevens. Surely this must be a monster.

He told them to call him Sarge, and everyone did right away. They liked the sound of it. It rolled off the tongue easier than "Mister Fitzweiler." And then Roy spoke, slowly and in a kind of drawl, about how the trustees thought it might be a good idea to take a little camping excursion to get to know one another.

All the boys agreed with Sarge.

And then Roy said not to mind him that he would be a . . . an advisor this weekend. Yeah, that was it, an advisor. Reverend Blake had told them that they were a good bunch of boys, and so he was just going to sit back and see how they operated. Derek relaxed and exhaled.

So they all met Friday evening in the parking lot by the church van, as they had done many, many times with Fitzweiler. They anticipated all week because they remembered Fitzweiler. Camping trips were his pilgrimages. He led his boys into the shrine, and there they followed and listened and nodded as he pointed to the glories and imparted wisdom: a khaki processional led by the holy hat of Bradley.

A station wagon pulled up by the side door, and Roy got out dressed in jeans and plaid shirt. He wore army boots whose shine would never be reclaimed. The boys tried not to stare, but some could not help it. No color. No magnificence. Not even a hat.

The sun slipped between the pines, and the campfire grew that much brighter. Dinner was done and over, and the business of setting up camp had deteriorated once again into the uneasiness of a stranger among them.

"What's next, men?" In the wilderness Roy's voice sounded like a very low-pitched scream. Everyone jumped, as if Roy had talked for the first time. A flock of birds bolted from a nearby bush and circled once over the clearing before flying out over the lake. Now, as if they had ever doubted, they were truly alone—and without Fitzweiler. Eric was more horrified than ever, but he didn't know why. He kept quiet as usual, ever watchful of Roy, trying to catch one clue (however minute) to make his first inhuman impression somehow legitimate. A flaw, a twitch, a quirk, at least a pair of bolts protruding from Roy's neck.

Derek finally responded. He liked being in charge and included in any group called "men."

"Well, we sometimes sing a song. Or sometimes Mr. Fitzweiler took us on a nighthike."

"A nighthike, huh?"

"Yessir. We enjoyed that a lot because Mr. Fitzweiler knew all there was about the outdoors." Other boys nodded.

"Izat right?"

"Yessir," said Derek, thinking he might have touched Roy's interest, "bird calls, insect sounds—Mr. Fitzweiler could imitate them all."

It was true. Fitzweiler was a man of immense and generous practical knowledge: plotting courses by the stars, semaphore, morse code, estimating the height of a tree, making plaster of paris casts of animal tracks, the difference between scotch, white, and pitch pines, leather belt handicrafts, and basket weaving. And though the troop was young and easily impressed by ranger hats and knee socks with tassles, Fitzweiler was still a very great teacher.

"Or sometimes he told stories he learned when he was young or when he was in the war."

"Were you in the war?" Steve asked the question that had been on everyone's mind. It was then that Eric realized that this was the thing he had been dreading all day long, maybe longer. Anticipated, waited, dreaded: the inevitable since Roy walked into the Grotto last Tuesday night. Roy himself shifted his weight to his other side and stared deeper into the fire.

"I was in a war. Maybe not the war you all are thinking about. Maybe not the war Mr. Fitzweiler liked to talk to you about." The fire spit sparks, attempting an escape from Roy's gaze. "Shit, yes. I was in the war."

One of the Tenderfoots let slip a gasp, a gasp the others managed to hold in, though they couldn't restrain their stares. Not only had Fitzweiler never sworn, he talked in hushed tones in the woods. Roy might as well have farted in the Sistine Chapel.

He began to speak. About how he arrived fresh out of basic training and was put in a patrol his first night in Vietnam. About how the five other rookies he landed with didn't see the next morning. About how they came up missing one by one, only to be found later in the night ahead of the patrol and in various stages of mutilation. About how he survived alone among the five, survived to talk about it. Eric thought, no, no, I don't want to go with you; I don't want to take this patrol with you. But he could not enunciate, and before he could protest further, he was beside Roy on the thick jungle trail.

"Once we took a jaunt into Cambodia to track down a squad of Cong. Supposed to be a get in/get out job. Like a walk in the park. Took us just a half day to get across the border. Pretty easy really because, you see, there ain't nothing that don't leave tracks. Spring, I remember. Orchids on the vines. Leaves real crisp and green. And then around noon the trail stopped and the jungle cleared and there was a temple in front of us, standing by itself as awesome as anything. Been there a while because the jungle had started to wind in and out and around the pillars and doors and windows. But still standing. And sturdy. Big oak doors in front. We knocked and were let in—just as simple as that, like selling Avon. Seems it was a monastery now, at least that's what they called it. Me and the lieutenant went in alone, and the place went on for miles. We couldn't even see the end of some halls and barely make out the ceilings of some rooms. And the monks—there must have been hundreds. Black robes, shaved heads, pacing this way and that, up and down the halls and across the huge rooms. I couldn't count them all. They wouldn't keep still.

"The lieutenant asked the head man if he'd seen the Cong or heard anything about them. Of course, he hadn't, just gave us a smile stretching across that damned serene bald head. I took the lieutenant aside and said, 'Listen, I can smell weapons here. They have weapons here. I know it.' He just said, 'Bevens, you've been out here too long.' Like he always said when he knew I was right. But that night I got a couple guys and turned the place upside down inside out wrongside up. We never found the stuff, but we knew it was there. At least we ruined all the hiding places. Not a vase standing, not a door still on its hinges. We did a good job alright. Yes we did. Like to go back someday and ask them where it was. That's all—just ask.

"The next morning there's three men missing. Someone said they were wandering around the outer wall. Well, we found them. On the edge of the jungle, draped over some limbs, away up in a big old tree, like ornaments at Christmas."

He talked slowly in a painful way of drawing each word out; not enunciating, not to communicate thoughts. He talked slowly so you would listen and pay attention, not because of the meaning of the words. He talked slowly to draw the listener out and on to the trail beside him, stretch the listener into his world to experience his pain.

"We got out and got out fast. Tore down the trail like hell. Toward the border. Dodging branches, leaves cutting us, skinning us alive. I still got the scars." He pulled at his collar, revealing a series of long red scars on his neck. "But we had to slow down. If we didn't, we would have been decapitated right there. About 20 of us left, 10 in front of me, 10 behind. By the time we slowed down, I looked behind me and there were only two left.

"And then the trail stopped. Just ended. Was there the day before. Was there when we went in. Maybe we got on the wrong trail. Hell, I don't know. Hard to tell. I heard the lieutenant screaming orders up ahead, telling everyone to shut up and sit tight. So I turned to my two guys to tell them to get on their asses and freeze and they weren't there."

Roy talked on, and the fire jumped in his eyes. About how the jungle moved that day. And how even the orchids on the vines weren't the same. How they all felt like roaches, those men squatting there in the dirt in the bushes. Eric heard water running very lightly and steadily. Was there a brook nearby? Could they escape that way? He turned to Derek next to him and saw that he was gaping wide-eyed and slack-jawed like the rest of the boys. Except that Derek was peeing his pants. But Derek didn't notice or seem to. The stain grew bigger and bigger until the front of his khaki pants darkened completely. It was so funny, Eric thought later, he forgot to laugh. He was scared shitless himself. The sergeant talked on, and the fire jumped in his eyes.

"And then what happened?" a tenderfoot asked.

"We got out."

The boys waited. But Roy rolled over and pulled his sleeping bag up around him.

"But how?!" Steve blurted.

"Can't remember." said Roy, already half asleep and speaking to somewhere down in the ground. "Can only remember getting in things, not getting out. That's the way it was over there. Better get some sleep, men."

No one payed much attention to Derek after the campfire Friday night—though everyone had been watching Roy all the time, and Eric was sure he was the only one who had seen Derek. But Derek was not the leader anymore. You could see it by the way he curled up in his sleeping bag and the way he sat and the way he stood around the next day. Urine washes away a lot of pretensions.

They spent Saturday morning clearing away a tree that had been lying at the edge of the lake for years. The camp ranger had suggested to Roy that it might be a good project for the boys. But when they broke out the axe, it was Roy who grabbed hold and started chopping with a fury. The boys gathered sticks and limbs, trying to avoid Roy's wide swath. He talked as he chopped, talked as he did the night before, in slow painful phrases, between each blow of the axe.

"Once, on a patrol, we hit a pretty fair trail for us—nice and wide and on the edge of a ridge where we could get some good sun. Just zipping along until all of a sudden there's this big, I mean huge, tree standing in the center. The path split on either side and then joined again. The other guys just went around it. But I stood there. I don't think they even noticed it. But I did, sticking up there all high and mighty. I don't know how they could do that." And he stopped and looked across the lake like he still couldn't believe it. And then he started swinging again.

"You know, I can't remember if I saw the top or not. It was that high. I just noticed the bottom because that was in my way. The limbs didn't start till 50 feet up. I took out my machete and gave the tree a hack. Not even a dent, just a little skin off the side. It had the blackest bark I've ever seen. Black and smooth and oh so hard. I hacked it a couple more times but nothing. Had a grenade with a wire, so I strapped it around the trunk and let loose. That took a chunk out of it, but only about as big as a baseball. And that wood inside was as black as the bark. So I'm about ready for a couple more charges when that damned lieutenant calls. I could have shot him right there. So I left it standing. Like to go back there someday. See that tree. Just see it. The tree and those monks. Wonder what kind of wood that was? This here's just beech. An old dead beech tree."

And then the tree was gone. Only the huge stump was left, so they wrapped a chain around it. "We'll get the ranger and his four-wheel drive to drag this thing out of here before we leave tomorrow. Yessir, if he wants it out so bad he can do it himself. I got another job for you men."

The boys usually identified flora before Saturday lunch. But that was with Fitzweiler. Someone mentioned the routine; Roy said, "Fitzweiler's gone, boy. I'm here. That old man's sitting in the Home right now pushing custard past his gums." So they all got out their portable packable collapsable shovels and started digging.

By noon they had all dug in, piling the dirt in front of their trenches. Branches, brush, vines were cut and stuck in the dirt in front for cover. Roy paced back and forth, surveying the work.

"You men gotta dig deeper than that. That'll barely cover your ass." The Tenderfoots were having fun with it: this was the first chance to use their shovels. Steve muttered throughout, but dug his twice as deep as anyone else. With Fitzweiler gone, there was nothing to stunt the full bloom of Steve's cynicism. He railed and swore and scoffed at Roy and loved all of it. He saw in Roy both a target and a prize, something to shoot for either way. The rest of the boys dug, not quite sure of their task and even less sure of Roy. By noon the edge of the woods had been converted into a series of intricate trenches that looked out from the trees, out across the lake.

At lunch they opened several cans of Dinty Moore and sat around eating out of their scout mess kits, which resembled sets of puzzling Chinese boxes. The boys were feeling a bit more comfortable around Roy now, though he was a much more imposing figure than Fitzweiler and made them do strange and unconnected things. But he was much more interesting to watch than the highly accountable Fitzweiler. Roy sat on a log and ate right out of the can of Dinty Moore and was silent. The boys chattered among themselves to fill the void. Neal and Rick started their game again. Steve tried to bum a cigarette from a tenderfoot he was convinced had a carton in his knapsack. Derek stared down into his lap. Someone asked someone else if his parents were going to pick him up at the church tomorrow.

"Parents?! Jesus!" Roy scoffed so hard a piece of stew skipped out of his mouth and landed in Derek's lap. Derek jumped and flicked it away as if it were a dismembered body part. Everyone stopped eating, utensils in mid-air.

"Parents? Do you think they give a shit what happens to you? They send you out in the middle of nowhere. They don't care. In fact, they make money off it. Didn't know that, did you? Fat cats. Rent your room out while you're gone. Have other kids come to the house. Try them out. See if they like them better. Maybe you get your old job back, maybe you don't. You don't know. How can you, out here with nothing to connect you back? No ties. Sometimes you float free, sometimes you swirl so hard it makes you puke. Don't know where you've been. Don't know where you're going. You just live." He pointed his fork at Steve for accent and then swept it around the circle, taking all the boys in. "That's where you've been, that's where you are, that's where you're going. Just living. That's it. And hope you don't trip no wires. Parents? Hell no. Don't count on them. They probably set the wires up, set the charges, climbed the tree to watch you skipping by." He scoffed again and started shoveling in the stew.

Saturday afternoons were legend in Troop 303, due solely to Fitzweiler's game. And it was a marvelous game of Capture the Flag that Fitzweiler presided over. From a small rise, a picnic table, a tree, he guided his army, pulled and tugged strings, gracefully swept them into position. He could see the X's and O's and reds and blues clearly, the arrows and fronts perfectly. With his binoculars dangling around his neck, his feet set firmly apart, Fitzweiler was an amazing man. And then he would switch and command the other side, just so everyone had a chance to win. Once when he fell out of a tree and broke his leg, he had his army prop him up on top of an old outhouse where he directed his forces to victory. They played in the open fields on the north side of the camp away from the woods, where the openness showed the attacks and assaults in all their glory.

But nobody could find Roy after lunch. He had disappeared into the woods. So some of the boys sat in their foxholes and waited, thinking that was what Roy had in mind anyhow, assuming the trenches had some purpose. Others, including the older boys, went looking in the woods. Maybe Roy meant for them to follow.

They didn't realize it until they were well away from the campsite: they had never been in the woods before without Fitzweiler, and then always with a purpose, an agenda, something to be learned. How different the trees looked, even in just one day. More now like a backdrop, more like scenery. Before, the woods were everything—in fact, too much. So bountiful that Fitzweiler could not get in everything he wanted to say in just one weekend. But now, Eric, thought, they just seemed like a good place to hide.

"Aaahhhhh!" Something huge dropped from a tree up ahead, shrieking as it pounced on to the boys in front of Eric. Something shiny caught the sun. Everyone dove for the bushes, and when they looked up, Roy had Steve in a chokehold with a knife at his ear. He held Steve long enough for everyone to see and then released him, Steve stumbling forward. Roy laughed long and hard and alone.

"You should have seen your faces. Lordy, I want my mamma. Why I saw you coming a mile back. Jesus, you are the sorriest bunch of asses I have ever seen. Where the hell did you learn to walk? All bunched up like that. You're not going to get three feet out here." He pointed to Wally. "You, chucklehead, take the point. And the rest of you fan out and don't stick so close. You'd think you were dating. Jesus."

He pulled a bottle with a label from his back pocket and took a long draw while the boys watched. Steve leaned against a big oak off the path and clutched his ear. A drop of blood squeezed out between his middle and ring fingers. Eric felt so grimy he wanted to jump in the lake.

Back at camp they bandaged Steve's wound—only a shallow 3-inch cut below his right earlobe but deep enough to leave a faint scar. Those who spent the afternoon in their foxholes sensed a shift in the wind, though they had not been on the trail, had not seen Roy's ambush. It wasn't that the wind was so much different, just somehow wrong.

Dinner was fixed in silence and eaten in relief out of merely doing something familiar. Roy's differentness made them all feel as if they had been weather-exposed for 24 hours, which they had been but never seemed to notice before. The hope and thrill of last Tuesday night, of something new to be learned, something that Fitzweiler couldn't tell them, sunk into a funk. The sergeant had told them things they didn't want to know and shown them things they didn't understand but knew they would have to someday.

Eric stared at Roy, who sat at the edge of camp, drinking from a bottle of orange-colored liquid. Steve ate with his head down, self-conscious of the bulbous, clumsy gauze lump on the side of his head. The rest avoided looking at Roy and then Steve, Roy and then Steve, Roy and then Steve. The comfort of routine had burned away; the mandatory game of Capture the Flag, the flora and fauna talks, the tales of General Bradley were all missing.

The Tenderfoots began to cry, but Roy paid no attention. He drew longer gulps from the bottle. And then he passed it to Steve, who held on to it by the very end of the neck and stared into its orangeness.

"Drink it. It'll sterilize the wound," Roy said. Steve sniffed at the bottle and then turned and leaned over the log he was laying against and heaved. He scurried on his hands and knees into the brush and wretched while the other boys watched. Roy picked up the bottle and emptied it with one gulp.

They tried not to look at him, instead staring down between their knees, down between their feet, down into the ground. But Eric looked hard at Roy—hard without blinking, so Roy would notice. Roy got up and pushed through the trees to the lake, escaping the cries, the wretchings, the stare.

Eric followed. He had to keep watching: that simple. Or maybe the feeling was responsibility. Someone had to keep watching.

Roy avoided the place where the old beech had been and where the stump and chain now sat—gave it all a wide berth. He walked out on a skinny canoe dock nearby, a temporary dock built many summers ago that was never supposed to last this long. He sat down on the very end with his legs dangling over the side and alternated drinks from a new bottle with gazes into the starry lake. Eric sat down beside him as he was expected. He had never gotten this close to a grown-up before, never on purpose. He could smell the sweet rot of Roy's breath and the heaviness of body odor. Adults got that way when they didn't bathe every night. Every night: they had to.

Roy tilted the bottle toward Eric.

"Want a shot?"

Eric shook his head. Roy pulled out a small roll of paper from his pocket.

"Want a drag?"

"No."

"You're a real uptight kid, aren't you?"

He was. He was the most uptight kid he knew. Every inch he grew, every pound he gained, Eric tightened up more and more. At a very early age he vowed that he would never smoke or drink or get married (those apparently being the Big Three from what he could see). Neither would he wear a tie, learn to drive, shave, or wear deodorant. All were sordid routines of adultdom. Eric wanted no part of them.

Roy belched and then farted like a ricochet from across the lake. Yes, here was a monster for sure. He could touch the monster if he wanted—and he almost wanted to—but he didn't.

"That'll change. That'll change real fast." Roy took another long swig, some of the liquid escaping from the corners of his mouth. "I was that way when I went in. But I changed. You have to change, or else you die. When you get out, you go through what you did when you first got there. Out of the war isn't too different from in the war once you've been exposed. You're jumpy first, anticipating everything, watching too much. Then you settle down, become part of it, comfortable almost. Finally, you want something to happen and miss it if it doesn't."

Eric thought, the misery's just oozing out of him. That's what I smell. That's what I smell on all of them—the Misery.

Roy smiled. "I've got this kid. A beautiful baby girl who does nothing but coo and giggle in her crib all day and night." His voice died and he looked out over the lake at the pines. "And when I'm alone with her she just looks at me. Not stares, but moves her eyes all around, all over, just really soaking me in. And then I can't move. Like a statue when she does that. It's like she's trying to place me but can't. Trying to stick me in a slot that fits, like the one lonesome peg without a snug little hole. Try to escape that peghole all your life, and then she looks at you, and you know where you've been standing all this time."

He looked out across the lake again at the trees, as if searching. That's where he had gone that afternoon, Eric realized, searching for black trees and monks but found only beeches and pines and a few squirrels. That was his misery.

"God, I feel like doing something. Can't go to sleep this early. Maybe I'll run around the lake a couple times to get tired. Or, hey, you want to wrestle?" Eric got up and started walking toward camp. Roy kept talking. "Calisthenics. Gotta get tired. Gotta get tired."

It seemed as if Roy ran and puffed for hours. Eric did not sleep, not really—just drifted in and out trying to stay awake to watch Roy. And finally Roy did slow down, not out of wear, it seemed to Eric, but out of the misery that became too heavy. He slowed to a walk and sat down on the old stump. Eric drifted in again for what might have been a few minutes and then out again for what was probably longer. And then he heard a big chug, as if Roy had consumed the whole bottle with one gulp. Eric rose up on his arm and looked through the clearing at the lake.

The ripples signaled out to even the farthest bank, each wave becoming shallower and shallower, losing power in repeats. And then from the hub the bubbles stopped, and then started again, and then sputtered until with two final bubbles bursting into crystal tones, it all ceased. Eric lay there stiffly, looking not to the focal point or even the bank where Roy and the stump and the chain used to be but across to the other bank in dreaded expectation, like the plants and insects must have done millions of years before when the slimy creatures first dragged themselves ashore.

But for once the dread did not materialize, though somewhere from out across the lake a sigh echoed back, the sigh of an infant finally shutting its eyes in sleep. He rolled over on his back and exhaled up and out through the trees and eased down into his sleeping bag and woke that way in the morning.

Eric was the last up in the morning. The troop sat with red

eyes around the cold ashes of the campfire, waiting for each other to fix breakfast. No one suggested they go look for Roy. Eric didn't say anything as usual. He had to see the lake.

The water was quiet except for the light mist wavering above the surface. He stood on the edge of the dock and couldn't believe there were no bubbles, not even ripples. Roy had said that first night, "there ain't nothing that don't leave tracks." But Roy didn't. Even the stump and chain, proof of a last Herculean effort, were just images now, no longer visible to the surface world. Maybe when summer came and the canoe livery opened and the swimmers started in—maybe. For now Roy was eradicated. Those ledger facts, the bits that Derek had first shared with them, that was Roy Bevens.

And then Eric realized that Fitzweiler was no longer there, either. He should have been bigger than ever now. Eric tried to summon the image—like a lighter that spits and fizzles. But the Fitzweiler of his memory, slightly bent forward, resplendent in knee socks and tassles, ranger hat set parallel to the ground, wouldn't ignite. It had gone down with Roy, both sunk together, dissolved like cotton candy and effused down and outward. They were not granite after all.

It was frightening: as if a van had pulled up in the night to his garden wall and hoisted his statues over and out and away. He could easily (and had many times) maneuver around the statues in the dark like a blind man, sure of their placement, certain of their certainty. But what was to become of him now? He started to fret about himself—that startled and appalled him. To think that the world could affect or (did he dare think it?) alter him. What was to become of him now that the monster was dead? He looked at his bare arms and hands: no scars, no scratches; not longer, not stronger. No difference. Perhaps he would escape. Perhaps he wouldn't be swallowed into the Misery.

But as he walked back to the campsite, he could hear Roy's baby girl, no longer sighing in relief, but crying loudly for her father.

He built a fire and fixed breakfast for all of them, never saying a word because they wouldn't expect a word. Soon the red eyes disappeared, and the tongues loosened, and something resembling the normal condition was restored.

They waited till noon the best they could but still no Roy. Somebody said he was probably getting the camp ranger so they could check out. "Maybe he spotted something," another said. They all had their theories. The Tenderfoots huddled around the campfire, ignoring Scouting Rule #18 ("Don't play in the fire or you'll wet the bed at night.")

And then they heard thuds and rustlings in the woods. The ranger stumbled through the brush with his clothes dirty and torn.

"Where's your scoutmaster," he yelled, "and where the hell did all those holes come from?"

Eric sat down on a log and laughed, and the troop watched him straightfaced until they got tired of watching, and they laughed, too.

Reverend Blake took over the troop and talked a lot about how Adam was the first Boy Scout and Jesus the first Eagle Scout after wandering around in the desert all that time. And how Noah used what he had—a real survivalist.

When Reverend Blake said "survival" it had that spiritual ring of goodness that made you pay attention because this was useful non-school wisdom he was imparting, the kind of holy reverence used when Fitzweiler talked about the woods and survival techniques (like it was an art). The word wasn't dirty and grimy like when Roy said it. Reverend Blake put it on the pinnacle and lit it up. Roy would hang on to the last syllable and let it hang there on its own until it dissipated: "surviiiiiiive." Like a whisper. And then it was gone, and he could breathe again.

ANNE FLANAGAN

FAMILY PORTRAIT

The first thing you see in Grammy's house is the Cutter family portrait. It was taken when—well, when we were still a family. It's such a joke, Joe, my older brother, calls it The Four Seasons because we're all dressed for different weather.

Dad got the portrait free from a Kodak exec with an overbite. Another fringe benefit orthodontists enjoy. He forgot to tell us about the photo beforehand, just pulled up in the Volkswagen on a Monday afternoon and said, "Let's Go!" Dad is dressed appropriately in a suit, pink button down shirt and tie. The rest of us look ridiculous. I'm in white shorts and a T, hot and sweaty from tennis. Mom, back from an Amway meeting, is sporting a rust wool three piece, and her Super Salesperson badge. Joe was on his way to *The Mousetrap* rehearsal, and is in costume; bundled up for a ski weekend. All our colors clash and everyone looks pissed off, but Grammy loves the picture.

Every Christmas we go to Toledo for dinner at Grammy's. Even after the divorce. Except now we don't all drive there together.

Joe is a senior at Denison. He's got a car, so he picked me up at Kenyon and we roadtripped to Grammy's. As we enter the hall, her cat Patches leaps off the widow's bench and snarls. Patches has cataracts in his left eye; it's white and filmy. Grammy got him from the Humane Society. She's always telling him in a high pitched voice, "Be nice, Patchy, Mommy saved your life." Patches really doesn't give a shit; come within two feet of him, he draws blood.

"Joseph, Mary Margaret! Happy Christmas!" Grammy greets us, wiping her doughy hands on an apron.

"Merry Christmas, Gram, Dad and Mom here yet?"

"Your father is out back with Zac. Karen called; she'll be here at four."

Joe goes out back to see Dad and Uncle Zac while I help Grammy set the table.

"Eleven for dinner, Mary Margaret."

"No way, Grammy! Who's all here?"

"The four of you, your grandpa-pop and me, Zac, Laura, Laura's date, and two ladies from Saint Anne's."

Grammy usually invites some misfits from her church. This time around, it is a bitter widow and her parrot of a friend. In the kitchen, the widow delivers a tirade of how she got "screwed" in the will. Her friend's head bobs up and down while she tugs at her tight blouse murmuring, "Yes, Oh, yes."

When Mom arrives we sit down for dinner. Grammy has me set Grandpa-pop a place, but it's only ceremony. He's in the living room, asleep in the LazyBoy recliner. He's senile and sleeps all the time; on holidays we just move him from his bed to the chair downstairs. He's a seasonal decoration, like a wreath.

Mom and Dad sit at opposite ends of the table. Joe and I are side by side across from cousin Laura and her date, Paul MacBeth. Paul manages Club Cinema, a video rental outlet. Joe loves his name, and all through dinner keeps saying stuff like "Prithee sir, be merry and pass the butter." Paul laughs, but there's panic in his eyes. Cousin Laura clutches his arm, grinning maniacally and dropping innuendoes and double entendres as she fights to control the conversation.

If anyone tries to change the subject, which is Paul, Laura's voice rises in volume till she is practically screaming. It gives you a headache, but we all play along. Laura is recovering from her second nervous breakdown and no one wants the responsibility of triggering a third.

Uncle Zac eats like he's a refugee from Ethiopia. He's dishing up seconds while we're still saying grace. In fact, the whole group eats fast, as though the food will self-destruct in four minutes.

"This is great, Grammy!" Joe says, dumping ketchup on his duck.

"Thank you, Joseph. Have you made post-graduation plans yet?"

"Bound for Broadway, Gram. Pounding the pavement, all that jazz."

"Not Grad school?"

"I'm *done* with school."

"What he's going to do for money, he hasn't decided yet," Dad says.

"Paul is thinking of expanding, aren't you, Bear?" Laura shouts, her eyes flashing as she looks around for an audience. "He's got a huge list of members now and may open up a branch downtown! Then maybe he could invest in something."

"Don't trust the stock market," Widow warns. "Those Wall Street bastards'll screw you everytime."

Parrot agrees.

"I've made small investments in the past and done quite well," Dad says. Mom clears her throat. It's true that Dad's made some investments, but he's lost on most of them.

"This summer I'm going to try to make enough to support me for a year," Joe says. "So I'll be free for auditions."

"Where are you going to work?" Uncle Zac asks, mopping up gravy with his bread.

"He's got an offer from me to work in Cincinnati," Dad says.

"Mr. Goldman said he'd like to have you back in the Arlington Arms." Mom says. "You liked working for him last summer, Joe. And you'd save money by living at home."

"He could stay with me and save money too, Karen."

"I don't know what I'm doing," Joe says. "A couple of my frat brothers are going to Alaska. Ken says you can make tons of money up there. He can get us jobs at a fishery. I may do that."

"Paul's been to Alaska, haven't you, Bear? That's why I call him Bear, he's my big Polar bear!" Laura is holding Paul's hand so tightly her knuckles are white.

"How are things at Kenyon, Mary Margaret?" Grammy scrapes the plates, except for Uncle Zac's, which is perfectly clean.

"Great. I've just declared my major . . . English."

"Oh, really?! I still have that first poem you wrote me, Mary Margaret, remember?"

Grammy gets up from the table.

"Grammy, you don't have to get it, I remember."

Grammy leaves the room and returns with a Naturalizer shoe box. She searches through it and pulls out a yellowed card.

"Ah, Here it is! 'To Grammy on her Birthday.' "

"No, Grammy, don't read it."

"The sun shines today
birds sing your song
a song heard before.
It remains beautiful.
But Time is stronger
And will one day dull senses.
You'll never heard the birds again."

"Oh God!" Joe starts laughing.

"I was only ten."

"I think it's beautiful," Grammy says. "Maybe I'll frame it and hang it in the hall."

"Grammy, NO!"

"Paul has a huge Warhol in his apartment!" Laura claps her hands. "In a gold frame! It's the one of Marilyn Monroe in all different colors."

The widow brightens, "She committed suicide."

Parrot says, "No, now they think she was murdered. By a Kennedy."

"That poem is so morbid, honey," Mom says.

"I wrote it right after Queenie died."

Queenie was my first, and last, pet. A brown guinea pig with a gold tuft of fur on her head. I saved a year's allowance to buy her. The pet shop owner showed me how to clean the cage, change the water, and feed her little dry pellets. He didn't, however, tell me that guinea pigs need fresh vegetables daily. Queenie got rodent rickets or something that paralyzed her hind legs. She could still drag herself around on her front legs; she'd go pretty fast too. But that summer she got really sick. I was at tennis camp. Dad took her to the vet and was told she couldn't be cured. When I returned, they told me she died. I found out later that she had been put to sleep. Apparently, Dad didn't want her to suffer, but didn't want to spend the money at the vet's; so he and Joe put Queenie in a Converse box, cut a hole in one end, and attached it to the exhaust pipe of the VW.

Then Dad had Joe run the engine while he held the box. They weren't going to let me know, but Joe told me the truth on my birthday. I got really upset and threw up all over my new Barbie Dream House.

"What are you doing for the summer, Mary Margaret?" Uncle Zac asks, dripping hot fudge on the table cloth.

"Out, out damn spot!" Joe says, smiling at Paul.

"Like Joe, I can either work in Cincinnati or Upper Arlington. There is also this internship my prof told me about for a literary magazine in Montana, *The Big Sky Review*."

"Not working for Cedar Point again, eh?"

"No, I'm definitely not working at Cedar Point again."

Last summer I worked there in the Guess your Age, Weight, or Birthday for a Buck booth. The pay was good, but the people drove me crazy. And I hated talking into that stupid mike. One time this fat kid came up and offered me two dollars if I'd guess 35 when he came back with his stepmother. "She's real sensitive about her age," he said. "It'll make her day." Sure, I thought, that's a great idea. He came back with his parents. The lady didn't look much older than 35 anyway, so I figured I wouldn't look like an idiot for guessing it. After much persuasion from me, the kid, and her husband; she agreed to take the "Cedar Point Challenge."

She wrote her age on a scrap of paper and then I proclaimed into my mic "35!"

"HA!" The fat kid clapped his hand over his mouth like he'd heard a dirty joke and wasn't allowed to laugh. The lady gasped, then started to cry. She threw down her slip of paper and walked away; her husband consoling her and the kid lagging happily along at their heels. I picked up the scrap of paper: 29.

"You'll have to decide what you want to do, so I can set something up for you, Mary Margaret," Dad says.

"She'll decide when she's ready," Mom says. "It's only December. Now—anyone for more ice cream?"

After Uncle Zac finishes his second sundae, we move to the living room. Grammy makes coffee in the kitchen.

"Hey, it's time for Dad to wake up," Uncle Zac says. He rummages around in the stereo cabinet and waves an album in the air. "Here's the ticket!"

Uncle Zac puts the record on: Tchaikovsky's 1812 Overture. He turns up the volume gradually while we sit around watching Grandpa-pop. As the music swells, he stirs. Finally, Uncle Zac has the volume up all the way so the floor shakes and trinkets on the speakers jiggle. He stands behind Grandpa-pop's chair, conducting an imaginary orchestra. The cannons go off, and Grandpa-pop's shoulders jerk with each blast—his eyes blinking open and shut. As the last chords come crashing down, Grammy runs from the kitchen and scratches the needle cross the record. The music stops and Grandpa-pop squints at us; confused and disoriented.

"Good Morning Dad!" Uncle Zac smiles. "Merry Christmas!"

Paul comes from the hall with a video camera. "Film Time!"

"Oh, Bear's such a video buff," Laura screeches. "He's always taking movies of me, at *all* hours."

"Let's get some shots of the Cutter seniors," Paul says, gesturing to Mom and Dad.

Mom shakes her head. "Take the whole family."

"Come on, let's get the proud parents first."

"No, why don't we all get in the picture?" Mom smiles, but it doesn't reach her eyes.

"Oh, don't be shy," Paul titters, guiding Mom over to Dad on the couch.

Mom shrugs his hand off her shoulder. "Shoot the whole family, Paul."

"Now really, when was the last time you two had your picture taken together?"

"When we were still married." Dad sets his cup down on the table hard.

"Oh." Paul's smile is stuck to his face, like a mask.

"Hey," Joe says, "Let's play charades!"

Every Christmas dinner at Grammy's ends in a game of charades. It's inevitable. Except for Joe, I don't think anyone enjoys the game. There must be a law etched in stone somewhere: The Cutter Family Plays Charades.

Joe starts running around getting paper and pens while Dad forms two teams. The widow and Parrot have to leave because the fourth part of a 'sweeping saga' mini-series is on. Grandpa-pop is asleep again, so it's me, Laura, Dad, and Uncle

Zac vs. Joe, Paul, Mom, and Grammy. We all write down two titles and I'm elected to draw first.

I pick from the other team's ashtray full of papers. Joe has a second hand and cues me to begin. I unfold the slip, MEIN KAMPF—book. I open my hands from a prayer position, hold up two fingers, then one, and point to my chest.

"Mary, woman, me, I?" Laura says. I shake my head and hammer my chest.

"Heart?" Uncle Zac asks.

"Go on to something else," Laura says.

Right. I can't get "mine," let alone "Kampf." I grab a pillow from the couch and hug it.

"No props!" Mom and Joe chorus.

I hold the pillow out and put my hand first on the pillow, then on my chest. Silence. I keep doing this increasing intensity till I'm pummeling the pillow with my fist. I'm like that robot Lady in "The Stepford Wives" who keeps dumping coffee on the floor after she blows a fuse.

"My?"

No!

"Mine?"

I nod and drop the pillow. Yea, Dad!

"When You Were Mine, Mine Eyes have Seen the Glory—something like that."

Good old Uncle Zac.

"No!" Laura smirks. "It's only two words and mine is the first!"

"How many syllables in the second word, Mary Margaret?" Dad asks.

I hold up one finger and then just stand there. Kampf, how am I supposed to act out Kampf? Who the hell thought of it anyway? Maybe Paul is a closet Nazi. Behind me I can hear the other team whispering and crinkling paper.

"Well don't just stand there, do a Sounds Like or something!" Laura is crouched on the edge of her chair. "Come on!"

What a bitch!

"Mary Margaret! Mine what? Mine what?!"

When this family plays charades it's not for fun, it's for blood.

"Time." Joe calls.

I sit down as the other team shouts "Mein Kampf!" and Laura gives a detailed description of all the ways one could act out Kampf.

Grammy goes next, then it's Dad's turn. He unfolds his title, reads it, and then turns around to the other team.

"Who wrote this?"

"What are you doing? Act it out for us!" Laura says.

"Joe, did you write this?"

"What are you talking about?"

"The title, very clever Joseph."

"What title?"

"*The War Between the Tates,* and I wrote it," Mom says. "It's a good novel, true to life."

"Nice, Karen . . . nice." Dad refolds the slip and tosses it on the coffee table. "I'm going for a walk." He slams the front door.

"Are we supposed to keep playing?" Paul asks.

"I've had enough of games." Mom starts gathering empty coffee cups.

Before we leave, Paul takes a photo of everyone for Grammy's album.

Joe is going skiing with his frat buddies for the week. Since I'm spending the week with Mom, Dad and Joe transfer my stuff to her car.

"You're all set Mary Margaret." Dad closes the trunk.

"Thanks."

"Now, I'll be down to fetch you Friday, right?"

"Yeah, you've gotta take me back to Kenyon Sunday."

"Fine. Love you." Dad gives me a hug. "When you visit, we'll go job hunting."

"OK, but I'm really interested in this internship. If I get it, I was thinking that maybe everyone could come to Montana in August to visit. For a couple of weeks, a vacation out West . . . like we used to."

Mom and Dad are staring at me strangely. Joe laughs. "You've got to be kidding."

"No—I just thought, it's so beautiful out there and—"

Joe shakes his head. "Sorry."

Dad touches my shoulder. "It would be difficult to get away . . ."

"Never mind, it was just an idea. A dumb one—forget it." I

get in the car and wait for Mom, who is staring at the pavement. Joe gives her a hug and hands her my backpack. She talks to him a second, then gets in and starts the engine.

"Seat belt, Mary Margaret."

Mom backs out of the driveway, just missing the fire hydrant. She doesn't say anything, so I turn on the radio.

"Is that too loud?"

"No." She faces straight ahead.

"Mom, I'm sorry about what I said. I didn't mean to cause trouble."

"Oh, Mary Margaret, you didn't. Really, it's OK."

But it's not OK. Mom won't look at me and her chin is quivering.

"I'm sorry, Mary Margaret, I am so sorry."

"For what?"

Mom shakes her head. There are tears in her eyes. Our headlights illuminate a bit of the highway. I turn to the window and stare at the passing lane, the yellow line broken up into segments that go on forever.

JOHN O'CONNOR

CALLABAN'S LIEUTENANTS

Marine Captain Callaban held a human skull in his hand. His thumb, index and middle finger poked through the top of the head. With his arm down to the side, the veins bulging in his arm, he looked like some mad bowler sporting a jar-head hair cut, ready to throw a strike. We were his pins.

I was sitting in the front row, alone. A mistake. The Marine had an eye on me.

"I don't think your mother wants your little butt in the Army," he said. He was staring at me. "In fact, you don't look like you want to be here."

I didn't but lied. "Sir, I want to be here. The only other place I'd rather be is in an M-60 A-3 kicking some ass with my platoon."

He paced in front of me, stopped, made a sort of right-face, lifted the skull straight over his head then thrust it into my face. "What is our goddamn friend Chernobyl saying to you Lieutenant?"

"Sir. He's telling me he wants his commy-ass kicked, Sir!" That was the answer he wanted. He had trained us to say what we were saying. It seemed stupid. No one argued. He kept holding the skull to my face.

What was I supposed to say?

The Marine turned the skull toward his own face. "What did I tell them, Chernobyl?"

"Sir," I said, realizing I'd made some kind of mistake.

"Too fucking late, Murphy," he said.

"Bandits Sir!" I yelled. That's what Captain Callaban called all the Army lieutenants who trained with him and his Marine assistant, Sergeant Powell. The reason the Marines trained Army lieutenants was the Marines didn't have enough money for an Armor School. Some trained here, some taught, and they had their own Marine-way of getting a point across. Sergeant Powell strolled up next to Callaban. Powell took the skull, smiled at me. Lieutenant Chernobyl had served his purpose. Callaban left the room. Sergeant Powell discussed the next day with us.

"All right, fellas, just like the Captain said: Lieutenant Samsa will be the Platoon Leader for the road march out. Lieutenant Corso will be the Platoon Sergeant," he said. "Sirs, I want you to get out your maps. There's some last minute shit we have to attend to."

There were moans from in back.

With a pig snort of laughter, Sergeant Powell opened his laminated field map. We opened ours, individually. Sergeant Powell began dimming the room lights with what looked like a channel changer. We traced the markings of the road we'd take out, in four tanks, being led by Lieutenant Samsa.

Samsa had black hair, a mustache, and looked like some mafioso. In most classes he seemed to know exactly what was going on. Lieutenant Samsa was sitting in back of me. Slowly, the lights brightened. I turned to look at Lieutenant Samsa, to give him a smile of encouragement. He was picking his nose. He hadn't made a mark on his map.

"Take a five minute break." Sergeant Powell said. "This projector's got the shits."

I felt a surge, a quicker heartbeat. This was the last class I'd have to sit through. Four months of Armor School were almost over.

I got up out of my seat and moved to the door and stopped. "I'm going to miss you guys," I said. I was looking at the picture of Karl Marx above the exit. Lenin was to Marx's left, to Marx's right was a painting of Stalin, a bust. It was supposed to be Stalin but it sure didn't look like him. This Stalin, who was painted by a guy during the Vietnam War, had no mustache. On the right corner of the painting, in white letters, it read:

SFC Leanard
US Army, Fort Knox
1971

I moved along the back of the room where five display cabinets held five different models of Soviet Infantry anti-tank weapons. I rubbed my fingers over the cabinets as if I were checking for dust. "Ah, yes, Karl Marx," I said. "Look at these weapons. You would be very happy." I continued walking toward the Soviet Soldier display case, enclosed in glass. I knocked on the glass. "Ivan. Can you hear me?" I asked. I was talking to the Russian soldier-mannequins clad respectively in their jungle and desert uniforms. They were blond haired, yellow complexioned and seven feet tall. This was the enemy. Our enemy. Bigger than life. They were trained tank killers. They drank rusty water and spit bullets. The Russian infantry was to be feared.

I looked at the clock on the wall. It had stopped. I checked my watch. Already the break had lasted six minutes too long. The class was filtering back into the room. During the break, those who didn't smoke or drink coffee stayed in the room. I was thirsty and walked out to get a drink. You'd think the building had caught fire for all the smoke. I walked down the hall. I held my breath ninety feet down to the fountain and ninety feet back. Just as I got inside the "Russian Room" as it was called, Sergeant Powell yelled at me.

"Lieutenant Murphy, are you all right?" Sergeant Powell asked. I was gasping.

"Yes, Sergeant," I said. I cleared my throat. "It's just that I've been choking on all the shit that I've got crammed down my throat this past week."

"Chalk one up for the el-tee," Sergeant Powell said. He wet his index finger and made a mark in the air.

My comment didn't get the laugh or short cheer I thought it would. I sat down, blushing, embarrassed at my miscalculation.

"Let's get the hell out of here," someone said.

The projector's fan wasn't working. Sergeant Powell said we'd only have a few minutes to take down graphics, new graphics to map tomorrow's road march out to the training area. We were going North. It was a rugged, hilly area rarely used. The contour lines showed deep valleys, several trails along dangerous ridges and lots of trees. Lots of trees.

"I guess I've got to thread tanks through a needle, fellas," Samsa said. I turned around in my seat to look at Samsa. He smiled at me and elbowed Corso. "But Murphy here is a hell of a driver. We'll be okay." I nodded.

"We'll kick some ass," I said.

"That's the attitude," Samsa said.

"Just remember, Murphy," Samsa said as we were taking down graphics. "Just remember that we are bandits, Murphy." Samsa was imitating Captain Callaban. "Bandits *fight* the fucking Hog. They don't *ride* the fucking Hog." Over the radios we were to call the tank a "Hog," a "Dick," a "Shank" or a "Tiger." According to Callaban the tank wasn't supposed to be called a tank. Also, when we're in the field, our minds were to be set on "combat frequency," or "combat freak" for short. Powell shut off the projector. It was smoking. It smelled of burnt plastic.

"Has everyone got their graphics?" Powell asked. Powell looked past me to the Platoon Leader, Samsa. Samsa checked.

"Yes, Sergeant," Samsa called out.

"They're all yours then, Platoon Leader Samsa," Sergeant Powell said and dropped a quick salute. Samsa stood up.

"All right. Tomorrow at 0-five hundred, meet, with *all* your gear, in this building's parking lot. Remember. Boudinot Hall parking lot at 0-five," he said. "Platoon Sergeant Corso, have you got anything?" Lieutenant Corso shrugged then stood up.

"Make sure you've got everything. Make sure you've got accountability. That's the first thing. I want to know who's missing," Corso said. "I want to know what's missing."

"Tomorrow bright and early," said Samsa. "No drinking tonight."

I was picking up my pen, notebook, and I was trying to figure out what to do with the map. I hadn't learned, yet, how to fold a military map properly. I just folded it and made my own creases. Samsa was talking to Corso about the next day.

Corso was saying how sick he was at all the red tape. Why couldn't they work out the bullshit in the field? The military, according to Corso, should be tailored like the wishbone offense. Corso had played college ball.

"The wishbone is pure. It's clean and direct. It's how you execute that counts," he said. I agreed.

"There's too much red tape in the combat arms," I said.

"Exactly. That's exactly what I've been saying since I got here. It's all BS," Corso said.

"I'd rather have a desk job. I could have gone Quartermaster you know," Samsa added.

"I heard Quartermaster's worse than this could ever be," I said. Corso nodded.

"No tanks though," Samsa suggested.

"Yeah, that's true," I said.

"No exhaust fumes."

"Well, not as much maybe."

"Some enlisted babes in your platoon."

"Some. Maybe. But you couldn't touch 'em."

"Better looking than the dumbfucks who are going to be in our platoons," Samsa said.

"That's the truth," Corso said.

"Have you seen some of the eggheads around here?" I asked.

"Really stupid," Samsa said.

"I saw a Corporal crash through, and level, the Burger King drive-thru," I said. "I'm serious. He was driving a new Camaro."

"You must have laughed your balls off," Corso said. I grabbed myself.

"I did," I said.

"How's about we go have a drink," Samsa said.

"I thought our fearless leader asked us not to drink tonight," I said.

"I did," answered Samsa. "I did so that we wouldn't be seen getting buzzed at the O-Club the night before the Callaban Show starts."

"Fuck it guys. It's getting late," Corso said. He tapped his watch. "O-five hundred and I haven't packed."

"O-five hundred and I'm not drunk yet," I said. "Are we ready to move out . . . Bandits?"

"Cut the shit," Corso said. "I'll wait until tomorrow for that crap."

We walked down the hallway toward the Boudinot Hall parking lot. On either wall there were pictures of Armor divisions from North Africa to Vietnam. There were pictures of soldiers crammed on tanks, posing. A caption read their division, battalion and company. It told of where they fought and where the picture was taken. Significant heroes had a thin white circle around them. Other pictures were more distant. Tanks patrolled Parisian streets. Tanks led infantry to bloody battles, through ambushes, over barren fields in Korea and Vietnam.

"Hop in, boys." Samsa said. Lieutenant Samsa was leaning over the pick-up truck's cab. "Let's get going." Corso got in the middle. I slid in on the end. I elbowed Corso.

"How many of those guys ever made it back to see their pictures?" I asked. "I wonder."

"I don't know the words of that song," Lieutenant Corso said. He didn't understand what I had said. He looked at me. "I think it's by Merle Haggard."

"Yeah," I said. "A lot of songs sound the same."

"Just shut the damn thing off," Samsa said. "It's only getting that AM shit. The FM's fucked up." Corso clicked off the radio. We cut through the Officer Housing Area, past the Fort Knox Parade Field.

"Do you think jar-head Callaban's going to bring that skull to the field?" I asked. We swung into the Officer's Club parking lot. Corso gave me a condescending grin, wrinkling his forehead.

"The head," said Corso very carefully, philosophically, ". . . is dead." Samsa brought the truck to a stop, cranked the automatic gear shift into park and turned to me. Corso hummed the first chord to "Ding Dong the Witch is Dead" from the "Wizard of Oz" and we sang:

Ding dong
The head is dead
The head is dead
It's really dead
Ding dong
Chernobyl's head is dead

We sang a refrain all the way inside the door of the Officer's Club. It was suggested by Samsa that Captain Callaban had never read a newspaper, much less a book.

"So how did he hear of Chernobyl?" I asked.

"He heard it on TV," Samsa said. "It's probably the only Russian name he knows."

"I bet he reads 'Gung Ho' Magazine," I said. "It's probably in there." We took off our BDU caps and strolled through a sitting room, past the dining room. Corso was walking in back of me. He tapped me on the shoulder.

"You think Captain Callaban's a fag?" he asked.

"I don't think so," I said. I appreciated the slander. "We could start the rumor though," I suggested. Lieutenant Samsa, who was walking in front of me, stopped. I stopped. Lieutenant Corso bumped into me from in back. There was silence.

"Well . . . what in the fuck do we have here?" Callaban asked. He was at the first bar stool facing the way we came in. "So the platoon leader is out with his platoon sergeant and driver. One day before battle." The old, white-haired bartender stared at us too.

"I came to write a check sir," Samsa said. Samsa pulled out his wallet and checkbook.

"How long you boys been here?" the bartender asked. He didn't wait for an answer. "You cash all checks up front, at the desk." He pointed up front then started wiping the bar off. Not for us.

"Thanks," Corso said. "We'll find our way." Samsa was still fumbling with his wallet and checkbook.

"See you tomorrow, sir," I said and saluted. Samsa saluted.

"Tomorrow bright and early," Lieutenant Samsa said. Callaban just stared us down. We left like scared mice, back through the corridor, into our hole.

"You, dumb ass," Corso said. "You're not supposed to salute indoors."

"I didn't," I said. I couldn't remember.

"You did," Corso said. Now I remembered. We pushed through the double doors of the Officers Club.

"I saw you," Samsa said.

"You did it too," I reminded him.

"I was just covering your ass," Lieutenant Samsa replied.

"Bullshit," I said. The truck was unlocked. We got in. Samsa backed out and peeled out of the parking lot toward Newgarden apartments, my home.

"I don't know why you live in that roach hotel," Samsa said.

"Lieutenant Fish said he kissed, I mean killed a roach in his refrigerator," Corso said.

"I'll bet he kissed a roach," I said.

"I wouldn't put it past him." Samsa said.

"I heard Callaban bit the head off a toad in the field," I said. Samsa corrected me.

"A snake," Samsa said.

"I guess we'll find out tomorrow," I said. I got out of the pick-up. As I opened the entrance door Corso called to me.

"Hey, Murphy," Corso said. Then he imitated Callaban's voice:

"What's our little friend Mister, I mean Lieutenant Chernobyl saying to you now?"

* * *

"You Army green fucksticks. Your interval is fucked." Captain Callaban was screaming over the radio net. "Now get your head out of your ass, Lieutenant." Lieutenant Samsa was leading us through some thickly wooded, dangerous areas.

"Tiger one . . . I mean Tiger two this is Tiger one," Samsa said. "Maintain interval."

"Get the fuck off the net, Tiger one," Captain Callaban said. "He heard what I said. He knows what to do."

"Yes, Sir," Samsa said. There was silence over the net. It was Samsa's fatal mistake.

"You're dead," Captain Callaban said. "You don't address your commander as 'Sir' over the net." Samsa was silent. "Who's second in command in that 'Tango'?"

"Lieutenant Murphy is in the driver's position," Lieutenant Samsa said.

"Then that means he's second in command now doesn't it," Callaban said.

"Yes," Samsa said.

"Then I suggest he get his ass in the platoon leader's position," Callaban said. Lieutenant Samsa and I switched positions. He became my driver. My heart was racing.

"Tiger one, this is Tiger four, over." It was Corso, the acting Platoon Sergeant.

"Tiger four, this is Tiger one. Go ahead," I said to Corso. Then Captain Callaban broke in.

"This isn't a goddamn phone call goddamnit. You've got aggressors in your area. Enemy contact is likely."

"All Tigers, this is Tiger one. Assume battle positions," I said. All tanks moved on line to a four-tank front battle position. Lieutenant Fish then made the fatal mistake.

"Soviet *tanks*," he yelled. "Soviet *tanks* to our direct front."

"Who the fuck said *tanks*?" Callaban asked.

"I did," Fish said. I could hear the diesel engines of the vehicles that were playing the Soviet tanks crawling closer.

"Platoon leader?" Callaban called.

"Yes," I said into my microphone.

"Do you read me?" I knew what he wanted.

"I read you. This is Tiger one, over," I said, correcting myself.

"Do you know what your soldier just did?" Captain Callaban asked.

"He just sacrificed our position to the Soviets," I said. There was silence over the net. I could not see the Soviet tanks. However, I could hear their cannon blanks fire. The noise echoed through the trees, along the hills.

"You're right, Lieutenant," Callaban said. "Who trains these soldiers?"

"You do," I said. It had been a trick question.

"No fuckstick—the Platoon Leader does," Callaban said. "I hold *you* responsible." Callaban then narrated the rest of the battle: "Soviet Armor elements have overrun you. They have left you without medics, burning. All Tigers are dead," Captain Callaban said. "Shut the Tigers off. Bring your bodies to the back of the Tigers, *over.*"

* * *

All the lieutenants were in a circle, dismounted, listening. I was in the middle of the semi-circle, alone.

Callaban pulled Chernobyl out of his sack.

Callaban shoved Chernobyl into my face.

Lieutenant Chernobyl had a freshly painted hammer and sickle, black, on his forehead.

"Sir," I said. "You can fuck off. . . Sir." I slapped Chernobyl out of my face.

Callaban picked him up.

I was sitting on my helmet but had fallen off when I hit Lieutenant Chernobyl. No lieutenant moved. They were silent, watching. Callaban stood in front of me. Lieutenant Chernobyl was under Marine Captain Callaban's arm, looking the other way. I looked up. Callaban gave a grin. His eyes looked hollow. He was gaunt, like a prisoner of some war. What little hair he had was matted to his head, the cut uneven. He must have shaved his own head. I looked at him. I wanted him to put a boot into my chin. He didn't. He wiped the Captain's bars that were fading, a dull grey, on his cap.

"They don't mean much to you, do they, Murphy?"

I opened my mouth. No sound came out. Callaban turned and walked away toward his jeep and tent area. I heard someone, maybe Samsa, say "Oh my God." I could feel their eyes on me. There wasn't anything to do but run. I ran. I got to my tank. I was going to get my stuff and hike into base, turn myself in. Instead, I sat in the gunner's position deep inside the tank.

I went through every component—Component Check, Hydraulic Check, Thermal Sight, Range Finder, Manual Sight, Proper Lay of Target, Reticles, etc., and repeated their uses until Lieutenant Samsa, from the Tank Commander's hatch, called down to me. It was dark. I looked at my watch. A couple hours had passed.

"Hey Murphy," Samsa said gently. "Um, Captain Callaban wants to see you. Sergeant Powell just came by." I tilted back in the gunner's chair.

"Thanks," I said.

"Hey, listen . . ." Samsa was cut off.

"Lieutenant Murphy?"

"Yes, Sergeant."

"Captain Callaban is ready to see you."

"I know."

I squeezed out of the gunner's position. I pulled myself out of the Tank Commander's hatch, stepped on the .50 caliber machine gun mount and jumped off the tank. I splashed in and sunk in the mud. All that had happened since we dismounted was black in my mind much like the night was now. I listened for Samsa or Sergeant Powell, but they were gone, probably on reconnaissance. It was dark except for the little kerosene lamp burning inside Callaban's tent. I walked up the muddy hill to Callaban's tent. Again I thought of walking to base. I felt the eyes of the other lieutenants on me as I walked.

"Sir. Lieutenant Murphy to see you," I said. I was just outside of his tent. I couldn't see him. I smelled the smoke from his self-rolled cigarettes.

"Come in, Lieutenant Murphy," he said.

I unzipped the tent lining. I walked in.

"Have a seat."

For the first time I looked up. There were three skulls on C-ration boxes set in front of him. They were in a half-circle. Each had three finger holes in their respective heads. I recognized the one in the middle as Lieutenant Chernobyl. Callaban pointed at an Army-green plastic milk container next to me. He had his thumb and index finger on the cigarette.

"Please, Murphy, sit." He was pointing with the cigarette.

I sat. It was a meeting of the lieutenants.

"My lieutenants, Lieutenant Murphy. Lieutenant Drago to your left," he said. I recognized the name. It was Rocky's Russian opponent in "Rocky IV." He continued. "Lieutenant Chernobyl whom you know, and Lieutenant Gorbachev, my newest Lieutenant." Callaban smiled at his staff. He seemed pleased. He took a long, hard drag off his cigarette and smiled at the skulls he had laid out. "We have voted," Callaban said and held up a blank Article 15. "We have decided not to give you one of these for insubordination." He wouldn't be pressing charges.

"Yes, Sir," I said.

"Instead, my lieutenants have decided, with me, to give you a choice."

"Yes, Sir," I said.

"You can stay in the field and cooperate with us. Or you can pack up and hike to base tonight," he said. "If you hike to base you'll have to report to the Company area and stay until we're back from the field."

"Sir," I said. "I think I ought to . . ."

"Don't answer, Murphy. Make a decision," the Marine commanded.

"Yes, Sir," I said.

"You didn't understand what I was doing out here Murphy," Captain Callaban said. It was true. I didn't but said nothing. "Remember when Sadat was shot?"

"I think so," I said.

"I was in Lebanon then. I got the call. Do you know what you do when that happens, Murphy?" He asked and pointed at me. "You got time to shave one last time. You look in the mirror, Lieutenant. If you can't look in there and say you trained your platoon right, you're fucked. You're dead. They're dead." There was a pause, a cold, dead silence.

"Yes, Sir," I said stupidly.

"Do you understand, Lieutenant?" He asked. I nodded. "There is only one sin in the Military. It is the sin of the infuckingcompetent lieutenant." I kept nodding and stood up.

"Yes, Sir," I said and held out my hand. We shook on it. I was a million soldiers in one, taking an order. I was standing atop the ruins of cities, the bones of men, women, children. I kept shaking his hand.

"What the fuck is it, Lieutenant?"

"Nothing Sir, just thank you." I stood above the human wreckage of a thousand years. I could feel the tremors.

"Then stop shaking my hand!" My hand felt limp in his hand. I let go. On the tent hung a clock, hooked to a humming generator. On the clock was printed "US ARMY" in black letters.

As I turned away, I saw some exotic island, a beachhead. There were dead Marines, rump up, naked, and half buried in the sand. The second hand paused at twelve, clicked by. I caught the sweet smell of salt air and counted my paces out of the tent, one-two-three, into the sand.

AMY SCHILDHOUSE

ALYSA'S FATHER

That winter after my father died I was thirteen years old, and I pretended that Alysa Schulman's father was my father, too. I caught a ride to Eastmoor Junior High School each frozen weekday morning with Mr. Schulman and Alysa. Their family lived in the house across the street from ours on Harding Road. Mr. Schulman dropped us at the junior high on the way to his law office in downtown Columbus.

I got to know him because his daughter Alysa and I were the same age. We used to play together in elementary school, and our families became friends. Once we began junior high, Alysa started playing with her girlfriends, and I hung around with the other guys. By that time it didn't matter, because I already knew Mr. Schulman. He was the one who offered me the lifts, anyway.

I began my friendship with him in the weeks after the funeral. He used to come around a lot, and talk to me about fishing or baseball. Once he surprised me in my retreat behind our woodshed. He told me it was all right for a guy to cry. He'd cried when his own father died, he said, and he was even older than I at the time. No one could replace my father, but I told myself that Mr. Schulman was the next best thing.

Every morning I scraped the snow and ice from the front and rear windshields of Mr. Schulman's black Buick, parked in the driveway overnight. My lungs ached in the artic morning air, and my fingers burned inside my green wool gloves, as I hacked and scraped at the ice. No one asked me to clear the windows. I wanted to do it for Mr. Schulman.

"David, just the driver's side is fine," Mr. Schulman commented one freezing morning. "It's too damn cold to stand out in this weather for so long."

He stood close to me by the side of the car. I breathed in his mixture of cigarette smoke and cologne. I admired Mr. Schulman's soft, black overcoat (which Alysa had told me was cashmere and very expensive) and then looked down and saw how his polished black leather boots gleamed against the trampled snow on the drive.

"Don't worry, Mr. Schulman, I don't mind," I assured him. "In fact, it rather gets the blood running, you know?"

He shrugged, and got into the car.

Rather gets the blood running.' What a stupid thing to say! As I kicked the front tire with my beat-up work boot, Mr. Schulman seemed not to notice. He'd opened his *Columbus Citizen-Journal*. He always read the morning paper while we waited for the engine to warm up, and for Alysa to come out to the car. I finished my scraping and took my place in the back seat of the Buick. Mr. Schulman's wristwatch beeped at 8 AM. He glanced at it and frowned.

"What can be taking that daughter of mine?" He shook his head affectionately. "Thirteen years old and already she spends more time in front of the bathroom mirror than Rochelle."

Rochelle was Mrs. Schulman.

"Alysa!" he rolled down his window and yelled. "Get out here!"

Alysa sailed out of the house and glared at her father as she opened the car door. I thought she was beautiful. Her skin was clear and white, and she had dimples, sometimes even when she wasn't smiling. She had her father's wide, red mouth and his same dark, bushy eyebrows. When Alysa slid into the front seat of the Buick Royale, I glimpsed her narrow hips beneath the short blue ski parka, saw her swinging, dark ponytail, and felt the breath catch in my throat. She didn't turn around to say good morning to me, and I knew that meant all I'd see of her was that fluffy ponytail, bobbing above her long, pretty neck.

Throughout the rides, I kept my eyes of Mr. Schulman. He drove impatiently, his forefingers tapping against the steering wheel. He repeatedly glanced into the rearview mirror. Was he looking at me? He chain-smoked, pulling cigarettes from a pack of Marlboros he kept on top of the dashboard. Grey smoke billowed above his head. What was he thinking? Was he thinking of me?

Our trips always seemed magically eternal. The heater's fan kicked in with dependable frequency. Mr. Schulman kept his radio tuned to WNCI-FM, so the same hit songs or local commercials or Paul Harvey's hypnotic drone came over the radio. Once in a while Mr. Schulman and Alysa spoke, but only to say which parent would take the carpool, which sister's turn it was to set the table, who had flute or ballet lessons after school—that sort of thing. Mr. Schulman would ask questions and Alysa would respond grudgingly or belatedly, or not at all. The smoke from Mr. Schulman's cigarettes hung in the air like motes of dust in sunlight. I never wanted to reach the schoolyard. I was a willing prisoner in Mr. Schulman's warm Buick cocoon.

That morning, I hardly even noticed it when Mr. Schulman cleared his throat, lowered the volume of the radio, and said to Alysa: "I'd like to know the cause of your tantrum at breakfast this morning." Alysa stared out her side window. "Hon'?" he said. As usual, she ignored him. "Alysa Jane, I'm speaking to you."

Alysa turned languorously to face her father.

"Flute," she said.

"Alysa, what is that supposed to mean?"

"Watch my lips. I-have-a-flute-lesson-after-school," she enunciated. "Mom's going to pick me up after." She rolled her eyes. "It's Thursday, Dad, remember? On Thursdays I have flute and Beth has Hebrew School. But the Friedbergs drive this week, so you won't have to pick her up. Mom told you all this last night at dinner, *remember*?"

I leaned forward to watch Mr. Schulman pluck the coil lighter from the dashboard and light a cigarette. He returned the lighter to its socket on the dash. A few minutes passed as he smoked silently.

Then Alysa said: "You and Mom are really going to screw us over."

Mr. Schulman turned sharply to face her. "What are you talking about?"

"I know what's going on. I heard you guys fighting again last night."

Mr. Schulman braked for a red light at the corner of Elbern and James roads. I glanced anxiously at the rearview mirror, trying to catch his eye.

"We weren't fighting. We were having a discussion."

"Yeah," Alysa sneered. "Some discussion."

Mr. Schulman glanced at me in the back seat and said, "Honey, let's talk about it later."

"I don't want to talk to you ever," she said coldly.

"Look, sweetheart, there are a few things we do need to discuss."

"Forget it."

"Actually, Alysa, your mother and I have been meaning to speak to you girls. There are some thing . . ." He glanced back at me again, ". . . we'll talk about at home."

"Dad, can I have five dollars?" Alysa asked abruptly. "I have to pay my French Club dues today and they're five bucks."

"Okay, honey—"

"Also, I forgot to tell you, Dad," she said, "Some man from the Temple Board called for you last night while you were out walking Jeepers. I told him to call back in ten minutes, but I don't know if he ever did."

"Alysa—"

"I think it might have been Mr. Sonnenstein, because he sounded familiar—"

"Alysa!" Mr. Schulman broke in, his voice suddenly loud and frightening.

Alysa bit the back of her hand and bent her head down to her chest. I watched her bring the other hand up to shield her eyes.

"Baby doll . . ." Mr. Schulman reached awkwardly across the space between them to touch his daughter's cheek.

Alysa jerked her head away from his fingers. She scrunched herself as close as she could to her car door. The traffic light turned green. Mr. Schulman drove through the intersection.

"Alysa, sweetheart."

"Don't talk to me."

Then Alysa was silent, hunched over and still.

Mr. Schulman was steering his big, wide car along the route we took each morning. I rubbed a clear spot of my steamy window and looked out at the familiar snowy lawns of our neighborhood. We were entering the parking lot of the junior high school. Pairs and groups of kids weaved between the cars and across the asphalt to the courtyard. Mr. Schulman waited with unaccustomed patience for them to move out of the way. He pulled up alongside the curb and put the car in park.

"Here we are."

Alysa jerked open her car door and leapt out of the Buick. Then she bent over and stuck her head back in the front seat. Her dark eyes were wet and glittering.

"I hate you!" she whispered fiercely. "You're ruining my life, and I *just hate you!*"

Alysa slammed the car door and ran.

Mr. Schulman, who had been staring at the space vacated by his daughter, looked up slowly into the rearview mirror. He squinted his eyes and regarded me quizzically—frightened, lonely, apologetic, strange—as though he had never seen me.

"She doesn't really mean that," he said.

I stared back at him, at his thinning brown hair and at the dark, puffy circles under his eyes. I saw his slackening jowls, and then I noticed how his overcoat bunched up in a fat, stiff, sad way above his seat belt.

MAJOR
OHIO FICTION WRITERS

ROBERT FLANAGAN

An Ohio native (Toledo 1941), educated at the Universities of Toledo and Chicago, Robert Flanagan now teaches writing at Ohio Wesleyan College in Delaware, Ohio. His time in the Marine Corps Reserves and during basic training at Parris Island helped him to write THE MAGGOT, "a strong, well-written novel" (PUBLISHERS WEEKLY) of Marine Corps life (now in its eleventh printing). He is a boxer and a poet, a dramatist and a story writer of exceptional sensitivity and strength. "Unflinching" best describes his treatment of life in the great Midwest.

Studs Terkel places Flanagan with the best of contemporary realists: "Robert Flanagan with these powerful stories joins Tobias Wolff as one of my very favorite contemporary writers," and his Ohio peer, Jack Matthews, praises: "The stories of Robert Flanagan's NAKED TO NAKED GOES are possessed of inventiveness, passion, and a wonderfully dense humanity. They are a pleasure to read and thoroughly admirable." His writing combines inner and outer drama in a direct and winning prose.

Flanagan has located himself in the heartland of Ohio in his poignant and provocative tales of the fictional small town of Olentangy. "I was born and raised in Ohio and it is my chosen ground. I love the flatness of my part of the state, its seeming dullness, the way you need to look hard at a Toledo street or a

Delaware field to find the beauty and drama there. As I wrote in an earlier story, 'Father's Day,' in describing the Olentangy River: 'It looked so flat and placid, so local, yet its hidden currents could drag the strongest man down.' That's what I try to get into these Olentangy stories I'm writing—that flat surface with something more at work underneath." The comparison to Sherwood Anderson is a natural one, but Flanagan takes his small town characters into the last quarter of the 20th century and into today's industrial decline for their struggles with displacement. His heartfelt characters are torn by love and loneliness, their values tested by the times which he examines with a humorous and compassionate insight.

In "All Alone and Blue" here we witness his unflinching portrayal of the war men and women fight daily for power and passion in their need for love.

AWARDS

Screen Gems Award for Short Fiction
Ohio Arts Council Grant to Individual Artist in poetry, fiction, and playwriting
Writing Fellowship for the National Endowment for the Arts
National Endowment for the Humanities Fellowship
Prize Story "Berzerk" in CHICAGO MAGAZINE
Prize Story "Naked to Naked Goes" in BEST AMERICAN SHORT STORIES

BOOKS

—Novels—
THE MAGGOT (Warners, 1970)

—Short Stories—
THREE TIMES THREE (Ithaca House, 1977)
NAKED TO NAKED GOES (Scribners, 1986)

—Plays—
JUPUS REDEYE (Produced at Delaware Theatre Ass., Thomas More College, Contemporary American Theatre Company in Columbus)
VOLLEYS: A CRUEL AND UNUSUAL COMEDY (Produced at Cleveland Public Theatre, Ohio Wesleyan University Theatre, and Ensemble Theatre of Cincinnati)

—Poetry—
ONCE YOU LEARN YOU NEVER FORGET (1978)
THE FULL ROUND (1973)
ON MY OWN TWO FEET (1973)
NEWS FROM A BACKWARD STATE (1973)
AT THE EDGE OF THE GHOST TOWN (1972)
BODY HOME (1971)
NOT FOR DEITRICH BONHOEFFER (1969)

ROBERT FLANAGAN

ALL ALONE AND BLUE

Spending Saturday night in a pole barn with the Olentangy AmVets wasn't Lee's idea of a good time, but Shelley wouldn't take no for an answer. Three whole months now they'd been going together, she said, and never once had he taken her to a square dance.

Lee could not do diddly with his feet to music, so sat watching Shelley sashay with bearded rednecks. She was a wonder at dancing, he had to admit. Nursing his Little King, he sat with his chair tilted back against the wall. He guessed he didn't look too out of place, and hoped not too much at home. His Daddy had loved these shindigs, but like his mother Lee steered away from them.

When he first met her, Lee had figured Shelley for a waitress or beautician, but never a teacher. She'd taken that as a put-down, but he'd said hey, no, he only meant she looked like the gals he'd known down home in Huntington. "You're from West by God Virginia?" she'd shrieked. She had gone to W.V.U. "Wild and wonderful," she'd said, "I love it." So how come he didn't talk West Virginny? He'd smiled at what he took to be a compliment; he'd majored in communications at Ohio U., he'd told her, and had worked his tail off to get rid of his twang. "Poor baby!" Shelly had laughed, "You worked it *all* off?" Thinking *home free*, he'd said *not quite all*.

She came whirling off the floor as the fiddles stopped, grabbed his Little King, drank, and wiped her mouth, "Woo!"

"You're hot."

"I am, son."

A left front tooth, chipped at one corner, gave her grin a knowing slant. Her brown eyes flashed with light. Why couldn't she admit she was a real knock-out? He loved that kick, sunshine or moonshine, she could give him. It scared him. Taking back the bottle, he put his mouth where hers had been.

The fiddlers scraped at their strings. Shelley fidgeted, looking to the stage. Even in bed her body quivered like a horse that might take off at any moment. Someone called to her and she backed away from Lee. "Come on," she said. "Introduce me. You'll give it some class."

He shook his head. "Here, I'm just one of your fans."

"All right! I love it."

She joined a couple of beef-jerky grandmas to do "Banks of the Ohio." Shelley amazed him. A Jewish optometrist's kid from Columbus, she sang that nose music like a born ridgerunner.

When she came down from the stage, people crowded around to slap her on the back or butt. Lee tugged at her arm. "Take me home, please."

She handled his Fiero with a flair that was beyond him, downshifting into curves and punching it hard coming out. Lee knew his brakes needed relining. A cold wind whistled at the rolled-up windows. He wore his seat belt and harness. The winding back road ran close beside the Olentangy where between trees he caught the silver flicker of the full moon on dark, cold water. The November chill seemed to go right to his bones. He hugged to his chest a cardboard box holding demo tapes, WCOL T-shirts and bumper stickers, some underwear, and his telescope. He'd been bringing odds and ends over the Shelley's all week. Sort of easing into things.

Shelley lived five miles south of Olentangy on a Liberty TWP side road in a place she was buying with a down payment from Daddy and a mortgage from BancOhio. Flanked by poplar windbreaks, the little stone house backed onto a sweet-corn field and woods. It had been built a hundred and more years ago as a school for mill workers' kids. Directly across the road from it the spinning mill, four stories of tumbling grey limestone, stood roofless on the river's east bank. Like most of the old Olentangy mills, it had been gutted by the fire it needed to keep going. It was posted now with *No Trespassing* and *Keep Out* warnings. Shelley said it looked romantic with the moon showing through its arched windows, but everybody who'd ever had anything to do with the life of the place was long dead and gone, and Lee found the emptiness hard to take.

As the car slid to a stop in the gravel drive, Sassy came on the run. "You been chasin all day?" Shelley cuffed the dog's ears. "You happy?"

"She'll run away or get hit, you don't chain her."

"Never happen." She dropped to her knees, hugging the mutt, mud and all. "No way I'm gonna tie you up, is there, woman?"

The dog pushed into the house ahead of them. Lee put down his box, opened a Little King for himself and mixed Shelley a redeye—tomato juice and Bud—which she claimed to drink for the vitamins. He sprawled on the couch while she lit the space heater. When the phone rang she rushed to answer it. "Bonnie! Where have you been, woman? I thought you forgot all about me. Tomorrow? Sorry, but we got some moving to do. Lee, who else? Uh-huh. No, with *me*. Get outta here. Never happen."

"Take it off the hook," he said when she finally hung up.

"She can't believe it. About us. You know Bonnie, right? You met her at the barrel races, remember?"

"Was she the fat one?"

"She's lost eight pounds. She's real sweet. She said next thing you know we'll be on our way to the altar."

"I'm lonesome here," he said.

"Patience, son. I gotta pee." She went to the bathroom—a corner panelled off to hold toilet, sink, and shower stall—and closed the folding door behind her. He heard the hook snap into the eye.

The house was small and crowded, its front door blocked by a pine wardrobe, its walls old stone darkened by ages of schooling. The fireplace was sealed with new brick. Cardboard covered the back door where a pane of glass was missing. The stormless windows gapped in their frames. He could tack plastic over them, maybe put in a woodstove, and brighten up things with mirrored tiles.

The apartment in Columbus he had shared with Tish for nearly a year was carpeted and air-conditioned with recessed lighting and wall mirrors. Expensive, but they'd split the bill. Now that he was alone again, the rent was eating him alive. He guessed he couldn't blame Tish. A network spot in Chicago was too good a shot for her to pass up.

Earlier he'd thought maybe Shelley might like to share his place; not that he'd ever said anything definite to her, but it was something to think about. The Continent was what the ads called a prestige address, a complex built in the European mode, and Lee's third story efficiency was peach stucco decked out with black wrought iron balcony rails, blue window boxes, and *cafe au lait* awnings. But when he'd taken Shelley home with him one night, she'd hooted, calling it "Disneyland." He hadn't said anything, but what about her place? So what's this, he thought of saying sometime, the "Pioneer Museum"?

Not long ago he'd have sworn on a Gideon Bible that he wouldn't be caught dead in a shack in the sticks. But it was silly for them to keep up two places, all the time they spent together.

Shelley came out of the bathroom and put a record on the stereo: blues harmonica. She was always playing music, and was always on the phone. Her post office box was jammed with mail. Her photo album was packed with shots of old boyfriends. Her dog went nuts over her, like the kids at her school. Neighbors called greeting across the field; in town everyone waved to her. Yet she swore she couldn't stand it when Lee was gone. How she noticed, he had no idea.

She came to the couch and lay on top of him. "You sure you wanna do this?"

"Here and now," he said.

"You know what I mean."

"Move? Why not?"

"Just making sure you're sure." She kissed him, then pushed to get up. "You're poking at me, son. Careful with that thing before you hurt somebody."

He held her to him. "You don't want to?"

"Not tonight."

"Why not?"

"You oughtta know."

"There *are* other ways, you know."

"Get outta here." She hid her face in the hollow of his collarbone.

The way she strutted about in public, flaunting herself, made her private shyness come as a real surprise. Now he thought of that shyness as her secret, one her admirers at parties and dances would never guess; knowing it, he thought, was a key to knowing her. He became lastingly patient. He did not demand. He wooed and seduced her each time as if it were her first. It was always no, then maybe, then sometimes yes. When finally she did fall open to him, her surrender excited him more than any of Tish's smart variations.

"You look great out there." He worked his hand beneath the waist band of her jeans to massage the small of her back. "You're all hot."

"Dancing," she said, "it'll do that."

"You looked beautiful."

Her full weight was on him; her hips had begun to move as if of their own accord. "You bring any bullets?"

From a pocket, he dug out a silvery plastic capsule. "Like a boy scout—prepared."

"Well," she said and went to the bathroom. He knew she wouldn't come out if the light was on, so flicked it off and lit a candle. He was taking off his socks when she dashed out to hide under the cover.

Her bed was a mattress on the floor behind a Japanese screen. As soon as he got in, she clung to him, her kisses wet. He worked on the sheath and let her mount him. The blade of her pelvic bone sawed against him. He loved to feel how needy she was, and how selfish in her need. He toyed with the black tufts in her armpits, billy goat beards, as he counted down and waited for his turn on top. Suddenly, she locked in place, face flushed. He gripped her arms tightly as she flared out beyond him somewhere, then eased her over. He was just getting his rhythm when she pressed a palm against his chest. She blinked, and focused on him. "Lee?"

"Easy," he said.

"I'm scared."

He felt her tightening up. "Don't."

"I'm too irregular, all right?"

"We've got protection," he said.

She put both hands flat on his chest. "No."

"Damn!" He let her slip away. She stared past him to the flickering shadows on the ceiling. The covers were a tangle about his feet. "Listen," he said, propped on an elbow, "you've got to do something about this. Sooner or later you've got to get over it." The very first time he had made a move on her she'd unloaded the whole story about Todd, her ex live-in, a bum who'd knocked her up and split. No way, she'd said, that she would ever go through that shit again. "Get a diaphragm, Shell. I'll pay."

She shook her head.

"It doesn't cause cancer, for Chrissakes, that's the I.U.D."

"You wear it then."

He sighed, heavily. "You said it'd be okay."

"I didn't say. I don't know."

"Sweetie." He slid a hand across her slippery belly.

"You ready to be a daddy, Lee?"

Sweat drying on his skin chilled him. Shrunken, he felt silly in the sheath. "How come you didn't think about that earlier?"

"I wasn't thinking, period."

"Why not?"

"You oughtta know, son."

"Boy, I don't know." He reached to hold her but she flinched and he withdrew his hand. He stared at her, coldly. Her big nose. Her chipped tooth. Her selfish, tight mouth. "Goddamn it anyway!"

Then her tears started and he flopped onto his back. He winged the limp lambskin past the candle and yanked up the blanket. She wanted to know could he understand. He didn't look at her, didn't speak. She couldn't help it, she said, really. "Listen," he told her, then didn't know what to say, then said, "Go to sleep. Okay?"

Curling against him, she slept. Just like that. He listened to her breathing and his heart rubber-hammering his rib cage and the dumb dog licking itself. When he rolled off the mattress, she mumbled, "Don't go."

"I'm not going anywhere, I keep telling you that." He pulled her robe from a clothes tree and tugged it on; tight across the shoulders, it ended above his knees. The linoleum felt frozen to his bare feet. He snuffed the candle. From the fridge he took a quart of vodka, knocked back a couple of slugs, then sat on the couch. The low flame of the gas heater looked like cat eyes. The vodka heated his stomach, the bottle neck cold to his hand. He stared at the folding screen. The mantle clock ticked. Why *did* she hold back with him? Twice now he'd thrown up his hands and banged out of there, driving back to his place in the middle of the night, thinking to teach her a lesson.

Sassy lay in front of the screen, head on her paws, watching him. She was a Coonhound-Doberman mix; bred, he figured, either by accident like most people or with the notion that the Doberman in her could kill what the Coonhound tracked down. But she had never gotten her full growth, except in the huge paws that made her look like a puppy still, and had turned out skittish. She shifted from scent to scent, never sticking to one long enough to do the job.

"Sausage, psst." All paws and no brain, she wouldn't come. He held vodka in the hollow under his tongue, felt it warm his mouth, then swallowed.

What in hell was he doing here anyway?

Lee had met Shelley in Columbus at a Leon Redbone concert. His station, WCOL, was co-producer so he got to handle the intro's. Eclipsed by Redbone, he was feeling low. Once Lee had dreamed of becoming a star—movie, TV, whatever. He had thought of it as bound to happen to him because he needed it so much, like other people needed food and a house. And because he had a gift, no denying that, a richly smooth maple syrup voice that carried him quickly onto the radio airwaves through hog prices in Huntington, the top forty in Marietta, a sports roundtable in Athens, right on to "All Alone and Blue," his own lonelyhearts talk show in the state capital, and then, to his surprise, no further.

That night with Redbone, Lee had noticed Shelley right off. Everybody'd noticed her. She was with three guys at a front table. (Brothers? Just good friends, she'd said later, and he'd kept himself from asking *how* good.) The four of them kept raising their Budweiser quarts in salute and shouting. "Leon! this Bud's for you!" Then Shelley jumped up to dance in an aisle, and could she ever dance. The house put a spot on her and the crowd clapped and even that old stoned fox Redbone tipped his white hat her way.

After the show Lee had caught her eye and said he admired her dancing. She couldn't believe she was really meeting him, she'd kept saying. Lee Peoples! *The* Lee! She always listened to his Friday show, but had never got up the nerve to call. He didn't know why she'd call in to "Blue"; she was way too pretty to be lonely. "All right," she'd cried, socking his shoulder, "I love it!"

He sipped vodka, looking out the window past a dime of a moon to Orion. Lee knew his heavens, yessir. Guided by stars he had always found a way home no matter how twisty the coon hunt trial or how wobbly his moonshine daddy. The right shoulder Betelgeuse, Rigel the left knee, and the Great Nebula, Orion's sword as Lee had recited for his mother, or maybe like his daddy said the old hunter's pecker. Lee's merit badge in astronomy was one among dozens; a terrific scout, he'd made his mother proud. She was a Baptist, born again and death on sin, and froze out his daddy for his every wrong—a freeze so common that although his daddy's brothers all spawned big families Lee was an only child.

The dog whimpered. "Sausage, you want out?" He got up and opened the back door. The November air was ice. The dog clicked its nails across the linoleum and went outside. Lee closed the door and put back the vodka. He lit a match by the face of the loud old clock on the mantle. Nearly three. He opened the back door again, and whispered, "Sausage," then "Sassy, Sassy." Nothing moved in the dark yard. His feet numb, he closed the door and tucked into bed.

When he sat up to strip off the robe, the covers came with him. Shelley was sleeping on her stomach. The fork of her thighs looked milky in the moonlight.

She was so deep in dreamland that he was in her and moving before she said his name. She tried to shrug him off. He braced his knees and gripped her shoulders. When she bucked, it drove him deeper. He heard her shout *no*, and stopped, thinking to let go, then plunged and was done. Hollowed out, he rolled away. "Shell," he groaned.

The first flare of light was the lamp coming on, red against his heavy lids; the second a starburst inside his skull. She smacked him again before he scrambled up. She threw something at him, a book, then a shoe. He ducked, and again. "Hey," he yelled, "knock it off."

"If I'm pregnant, I'll kill you." She had the blanket whipped around her, her throwing arm free. The candle stub hit him in the neck.

"You're not pregnant."

"You don't know. You don't care."

"Come on." He moved toward her, wary. All he wanted was to crawl under the covers, to feel warm and hold her and sleep. She pushed his hand away from her face.

"You know what that was? You don't know, do you? Rape!"

He felt defenseless, naked, and gathered up his clothes. "I can't believe I'm hearing this." One leg in his cords, he hopped to keep his balance.

"Rape, Lee."

He pulled on his white sweater and angrily slapped black dog hair from it. He waited for her to ask where he thought he was going, but she just stared holes in him. "What are we?" he asked. "Strangers?"

"Get out of here."

"Shell . . ."

"Out!"

"What about tomorrow, the big move?"

"Unless you want me to call the sheriff." She picked up the telephone.

"Hey," he said, "I'm not the guy who knocked you up, you know. You got me mixed up with one of your other bums."

She dialed. He tore his parka from a chair. His unlaced shoes flopped like clown feet. She held the black phone against her belly. "You half-assed hillbilly," she said.

"That does it!" He ripped open the door to the cold, and Sassy shouldered in, happy to be home.

The first time he had called her for a date, she'd asked if it was a joke. Out of all the women in the world—to pick *her*? It scared her to feel so happy. She kept telling herself he just figured her for an easy score.

Shelley stopped at the school door, one hand on the brass rod, her face close to the cold glass. Lee's red Fiero was parked out front. Great! So where had he been all week? One thing for damn sure, she wasn't wanting a fight. She'd been up most of the night, and had been snapped awake at dawn by shots and Sassy's barking. Hunters worked the woods behind her house. Deer, cows, dogs, nothing was safe. And for the sixth morning in a row, her stomach was sick.

Rafael, her hyperactive dyslexic, stood on the cement stoop just outside the double doors. He wore an open jean jacket and one red mitten. Spaced on Ritalin, he chewed a pencil taken from Shelley's desk. He stole her pencils, paste, crayons, and once her car keys. Even when she caught him red-handed, he would not admit to doing anything wrong.

The boy turned to look at her so. Flipping her scarf about her neck, she stepped outside. She pretended not to notice when he hid the pencil. "Your mama coming after you?"

Rafael nodded. His mother was half black, half white, his father Mexican. Shelley liked the couple because they held hands during parent-teacher conferences. And she felt protective of them. She knew the local yokels looked down on them as mongrels.

She put an arm around the boy's boney shoulders and felt him cringe. All day long he begged for attention, yet pulled away whenever she touched him. His fear angered her. Before letting him go, she fastened his jacket snaps. "Wanna carry my books, son? Wanna walk me to my car?"

"I do, Miss G." He took her bag, dropped it, and picked it up.

"How's it goin? You happy it's Friday?"

He shrugged. He had spent much of the day crying. When they colored the cut-out turkeys, he'd done his in solid black.

"How come you didn't turn in your homework?"

"I do, Miss G."

Lee got out of his car. "Shell?"

"You shouldn't tell lies," she said.

"No, Miss G., I give it to you."

"Wait up." Lee walked behind her. "Hey, come on."

When Lee had started dropping by the school, one of the aides, newly unwed, squealed "God, he's a dream! I listen to him all the time! I can't believe . . . I mean, you know." Sure, Shelley knew. Then, because the little groupie was drooling so, Shelley tossed her a bone by remarking that Lee wasn't all that perfect; he snored and hogged the covers.

Shelley unlocked her Bobcat, got in, and rolled down the window. "What are you trying to prove?" Lee asked.

"My bag," she said.

Lee reached for the bag and Rafael jerked away, dropping it in the street. A reading book and sheaf of papers fell out. Rafael jammed them back into the bag. Side-stepping Lee, he lifted it to the window.

"All right. You're my helper, aren't you, son?"

Rafael reached into a back pocket, and held something out to her. "This fall out."

It was a wrinkled sheet of paper. His homework. She took it. "Go on, Rafael, your Mama'll be hunting after you."

The boy moved off, chewing on her pencil.

Lee leaned in at the window. "Don't be this way."

She wondered if anyone in school was watching. She knew she was a source of scandal for the other teachers, especially the churchy married ones, and considered getting out to slap Lee's face or jump into his arms. But they'd seen it all before. If she ran him over though, that might spice up their melba toast and Sanka lunches.

"I keep calling you, why won't you talk to me?"

"Twice," she said.

"You hung up on me."

"Poor baby! You run out of quarters?"

"You know, sometimes I don't understand you at all."

"*Some*times?" She fired up the Bobcat's engine.

He hung his head, then looked up at her from under his cocker-spaniel eyebrows. "They want to know, am I moving or not?"

"That's all you got to worry about?"

"What's that mean? You didn't really call the law, did you?"

"Oh, that's perfect!" she said. "Look out or you'll get run over." She pulled away from the curb, missing him.

What she ought to do was to call up her square dance buddies Scotty and Trapper and have them kick Lee's ass. If she was pregnant, maybe she would. But no, she knew. She'd call Evie, just like the time before. Please don't tell Papa and Mama, please come be with me. And her sister, older, wiser, and pretty, had held her hand while they'd reamed Shelley with the vacuum, the clear tube flushing red with her blood, Baby Hoover, better to send it down the drain than to bring it into such a screwed-up world a bastard like its papa and maybe like its mama, a goofy-looking kike. She'd tried to scream, the pain was so bad and all they'd given her was one lousy little Valium, but her jaws locked open and all she could get out were little squeaks, like some damned mouse in a trap. Later, back at her house, flat on her back—"mattress back," Todd had called her— the pain draining away, she had promised whatever Evie wanted to hear. In the future she'd be careful. Like the other Gold women, she'd lock it up as tight as Fort Knox. We all make mistakes, love, Evie had said, the princess who'd produced two fine grandchildren and whose pudgy hubby, Bernie Klein C.P.A., was accepted as one of the Golds. Shelley had given up long ago trying to compete. She just hoped that Evie made up to Mama and Papa for their gawky and rowdy daughter getting stuck in the sticks knocked up by rednecks.

She gunned through Olentangy, hitting three of the nine main drag lights on the yellow.

At times, despite the AmVet applause, she couldn't quite shake the feeling that the locals lumped her with Rafael's people. Not that they were about to burn a cross in her yard, but there were the odd little looks, the things said or not said.

Todd, after their big break-up, ran into her one night at Trapper's. He was drunk and called her a stinking kike. Trapper said hey, cool it, but didn't do anything, Todd being a karate freak. She threw her redeye in the freak's face. She thought he'd hit her, but instead he announced to everybody what a relief it was to go to bed without those gorilla legs scratching at him. Shelley had stood her ground and taken it. Maybe she looked tough. She didn't have anything else to throw and would have missed him anyway with the damn tears in her eyes. He'd stormed out, leaving her to deal with his mess, his style exactly. Then everybody had tried really hard to pretend that nothing had happened, and not one person there spoke up in her defense, though she'd been standing right beside Doris and Scotty, longtime friends, and Trapper who knew damn well that even though she didn't shave them Shelley's legs didn't feel all that bad.

She should have ditched Todd from the word *go*. She'd tried to, really, but he'd kick open the door and they'd fight and talk and drink and end up in the sack. Until she'd missed a few periods anyway. That had been the end of Todd, which she'd called breaking up with him, though she knew she'd been dumped.

The phone was ringing when she opened the door. She let in Sassy and lifted the receiver, ready to hang up.

"Finally, I reached you!"

"Oh," Shelley said. "Hi, Mama."

"How are you *there*?" Her mother always said *there* as if Shelley lived in some unpronounceable foreign country, though Olentangy was only twenty-odd miles north of Columbus, the Gold home ground. When Shelley had stuck to it about choosing West Virginia University because of courses in clog dancing and hammer dulcimer, her mother had acted as if her daughter were being shipped off to Irkutsk. "You are coming home for Thanksgiving, aren't you? Your sister's family will be here."

Above her chewed couch hung a framed photo-montage Evie had made: all the Golds from great-greats down to baby Shelley. Petite and beautiful, Mrs. Gold was a lady, her legs like her furniture waxed to perfection. Shelley took after her plain, rangey father who, thoughtful in his way, told her hundreds of times in her trying teens (she tried grass, she tried sex, she tried running away) that looks were not everything. Yet he had married a looker, and paid through the nose to keep her in fashion. "I'll try to make it, Mama, all right?"

"It would be helpful to know who intends to come."

"Yeah, wouldn't it?" She tossed Sassy a sweat sock. "Look, I don't want turkey anyway. If I make it, I'll bring something."

"On Thanksgiving, you eat soybeans?"

"Think of it as my kind of kosher, all right?"

"Will you be bringing someone? Your new friend?"

"Could be, Mama." Actually, she wouldn't mind seeing Evie compare balding Bernie to Lee the dreamboat. "Soon as he makes up his mind, I'll let you know."

Off the phone, she mixed a redeye and sat cross-legged on the wood floor. Sassy pawed at her. She snatched up the sock and Sassy fought for it, rocking her head back and forth, eyes bugging out, a growling deep in her throat. "Hang in there, you sassy little bitch! You tough? You gonna give up, huh?" The dog lunged to lock its jaws in a closer hold. "All right!" She clasped the hound's head in both hands to kiss the black forehead between the worried tan brows, then let go. Sassy carried the sock to a corner, her prize.

Why is it you pick such unsuitable types? her mother would ask.

Mama, I take whatever comes my way.

At the start Lee had been so careful to make no promises. He was on the rebound, he didn't know about his future, blah, blah. Hey, all right, she understood. But it got to her. And the way he would sign his notes: L. What's this mean, she'd ask, Love, Lee, Later? He had said she was acting paranoid. But after that he would write Love, Lee. Which didn't mean a damned thing to her since she'd had to ask him for it.

In the bathroom she scrubbed her face. The mirror over the sink was the only one in the house, a small oval glass she'd picked up cheap at a flea market. She felt no call to gawk at herself. Her nose was too big, one thing. It wasn't as bad as her grandpa's beak, but it was prominent, maybe monumental; a Mt. Rushmore schnozz. She exaggerated, Evie told her. Yet really if it's such a bother, love, why not get it fixed? Evie was very pleased with her new nose. But Shelley prided herself on not being vain, thank you. She rubbed dry on a scrap of towel.

The chill in the house, and the quiet, made everything seem bleak. Was this how it was always going to be? Like at the square dances, when she'd watch the others spinning to the fiddles and seeming linked together body and soul. Yet when she joined in, she only felt more alone. She lit the space heater, and turned on lights and the stereo. "Everybody's looking for something," the flat bratty chant of the Eurythmics, "sweet dreams are made of this."

She took a key from an ashtray on the mantle, opened the glass face of the Ingraham clock from Olentangy Oldtiques and wound tight its two springs. What she needed was to teach in her own one-room school. If she had kids from the first through eighth, then she could see the difference, if any, she made in their lives. Catherine Marshall's *Christy* was still her favorite book, next to Anne Frank's *Diary*. And what she really wanted, someday, was a big old house on a hill with land enough for dogs and horses. And room for some kids. She could adopt, if nothing else. There were lots of kids around nobody wanted, *that* was for damned sure.

At the kitchen table, she graded papers. It hurt her to see how her class, the learning disabled, struggled to spell the simplest words. She did her best with them, giving out tons of hugs and kisses, and crying "I love it!" when they got anything right. And they loved her. They weren't faking it, she didn't think. Really. They hung one her, gave her kisses wetter than Sassy's and begged for trips to Miss Gold's house where they got cookies and punch, and played kickball and tag, and frisbee with the doggy.

She unfolded Rafael's homework. She had spent all week with him on his spelling. Not *god,* she'd showed him, *dog.* The *dog* ran away. Now, she shook her head in defeat. *Hurt* was *truh,* and *love* and *evol.* The paper was signed *Leafar.*

She'd spend her whole life in school, she thought, yet never get a clue to what she was supposed to learn.

Maybe if only you could say what it was—All right, you're alone. All right?—and give up wishing your papa and mama or sweetie who was really a prick would take away the hurt and make it all better, then maybe it was just one more shitty thing you had to live with, like acid rain or your period or slaughterhouses or brain damage.

At the refrigerator she took out the tomato juice, and was hunting among the Little Kings for a Bud when the half-gallon bottle slipped from her hand to explode on the floor. Bits of glass stung her legs. She looked at them running with blood, then saw it was juice, and instantly felt it cold against her skin. "Look at this mess!" she cried to Sassy. "Just look at this mess!"

She grabbed one of his beers, slammed shut the fridge, and collapsed on the couch. "All right," she said, "So you're alone." But it wasn't all right. It was all fucked up from the word go. Or she was.

God, how she wanted to hear that smooth sure radio voice saying "Shelley"—a name she'd always hated but that sounded like music when he said it—saying "Shelley, you're being silly. Your nose is fine, your ass isn't too fat, everybody is nuts about you."

Yeah, right. She popped the cap off a Little King. Evol eel. Here's to you, you prick.

Just when he thought they were getting to know each other, what'd he find out? She was nowhere close. Anybody who knew him knew he was an easygoing guy. His listeners loved him.

Lee couldn't figure it. He would never say so to her face, but really one of the big attractions Shelley'd had for him was that they didn't have to take each other all that seriously. Not that he thought of her as some no deposit-no return. Who was it kept telling her how good she looked? *She* never thought so. In fact, she had such a low opinion of herself that he'd made a special effort to get her out and around, to boost her ego. Lee might not be a big television star (well, he wasn't period; and the way it looked now he never would be) but he had his fair share of Buckeye Country fans and knew Shelley liked being seen with him, especially when someone would recognize who he was. Not that he was doing her any favors. To tell the truth, he got a real kick out of her, how excited she got about things, like a kid, and the way she played at being the country gal. But now all she did was find fault with him, like they were already married.

A guy could be too patient, too understanding.

But damn, he missed her. Her twangy chatter. That knowing grin. Her sailor's swagger and duck butt. She looked funny, yet sexy. Like a tramp, Chaplin, an orphan. She looked so loveable sometimes it about broke his damned heart.

Still, maybe what he needed was to make a clean break. Maybe he already had.

At the station the Mister Coffee was perking. Lee poured himself a cup, dumped in sugar and stirred it with a stick. Merri was setting up to screen his calls and he watched her long legs cross the room. Merri wasn't all that bright but she was agreeable, meaning she hadn't said no very often. How was it that such petty things as her saying "rilly" for "really" got under his skin so? She came from up around Marion and probably her daddy got home from work "booshed" and went "feeshing." Lee remembered the night at her place when Merri had been mad at him about something or other he had or hadn't done, and said to him, "You never worry about *my* fillings, do you." He'd told her to see a dentist. Then things rilly got bad. And they'd ended altogether when she pushed him to have Sunday dinner with her folks.

Merri sat at her desk. "Lee," she said, sounding surprised or maybe pleased, "you look rilly beat."

He shut himself up in a broadcast booth crammed with deejays' automated tape carousels. The engineer waved to him. *On the Air* flashed red, and he leaned into the mike. "All Alone and Blue. Lee here, just for you, every Friday night. Because let's face it—nobody wants to be alone. So let's bring some folks together, okay? If we can do that, the rest will take care of itself." He announced the number to call and drank his coffee during the commercial tapes. Then Merri was lighting up the buttons on his console and he began taking calls from people hoping to find a friend or wanting someone to marry or maybe just needing to get laid.

"Okay, Jim, let's see what's out there. You heard him, ladies. Jim's thirty, never been married, not yet anyway, and works in the field of night security. He likes bowling, and hey, he's got a mustache like Burt Reynolds. Have a heart. Give us a call."

After spots for Spa Lady and Waterbeds Unlimited, Cindy, Faye, and Peg were lined up. "So what do you do, Peg? Not a nurse, a nurse's aide. Okay. Tell us, how far's too far on a first date? A kiss? More than a kiss? More than more than a kiss?"

Lee tried, but there was no spark at all to his talk. He used to get a charge out of going on live without a script, to hook up with his listeners. By now though he could guess what his callers would say and, having learned what people liked him to say, had his part down pat.

"Peg, if your love life were made into a movie, how would it be rated? G, PG, R, or X? Hey, Jim! Peg says she's an X! You got three minutes. Get to know each other."

He leaned back in the chair and stared at the acoustical tile ceiling. His callers tried so hard to sound cheery, as if calling in were only a joke. Other people might be lonely, but not them. Well, not really lonely. Not desperate anyway. ('Hi, Peg.' 'Hi, Jim.' 'How you doin?' 'Oh, pretty good, and you?' 'Me? Super.' 'That's nice.' 'So what do you like to do, Peg, you know?' 'Oh, just about anything, Jim, really.' 'Hey, Super.') Why couldn't they come right out and say it? Listen, I can't stand being out here all alone, but I'm scared to death of getting locked into anything. Okay?

"Don't stop talking, Jim," he said to the mike. "I think Peg's getting interested."

Twice that week Lee had made himself go out after work. He'd had a drink with a redhead who wrote ad copy. She wore green-tinted contacts and talked at word processor speed about her investment group and the terrific aerobic benefits she got from power walking. Tish all over again. When she'd invited him in for a nightcap, he had begged off with a headache.

Next he'd gone to a neighborhood bar, one Shelley liked. A mounted buck's head, Swisher Sweets, and pork rinds: he could have been down home. While the bartender stared at TV, Lee had sipped Little Kings and tried not to watch a fortyish fat guy hugging the juke box and singing along, teary-eyed, with the Everly Brothers, "Whenever I want you, all I have to do . . . is dreeeeam."

A white light blinked. "She says it's personal," Merri said.

"I'll take it."

"Lee?"

"You got me, Shelley." He hadn't had any trouble filling his time before he met her; now all he had was time. "You call to apologize?"

"For what?"

"This afternoon."

"I run you over? I hurt your foot?"

"Not my foot."

"Look, I'm sorry, all right? I didn't call to start a fight."

"We've got one minute. I have to get back."

"I know. Lee."

"You sound kind of down."

"No. Oh, you know."

He craned his neck but couldn't see Merri's desk. "I know."

"I was just, I don't know, I was just laying here, listening to you. You sound so close."

"Lying."

"No, you do."

"You lie, you don't lay."

"You want me to go, say so."

"Shelley, you're a teacher. You should know these things."

"All right. I'm gone."

"No, wait. Merri, you on the line?"

"Who?"

"Nobody. Listen, I'm glad you called. Really. But, how come?"

"I told you. In the dark here, you sounded so nice."

"Thanks." Once when he'd brought her roses, she asked him if anybody'd ever told him he was a nice guy. Sure, he said, but later she changed her mind. They'd laughed about it then. "You having a few redeyes tonight?"

"A few. Maybe."

"You sound like it."

"If you mean, am I drunk, I'm not."

"Hey, no, don't get me wrong. Sassy there?"

"By my side."

"Lucky dog."

Jim and Peg were deciding whether to have spaghetti or steak on their first date. If they went out. If they had dinner first. There were big gaps in their talk. Jim wanted to know, if they had steak, did Peg like it well-done or rare.

"Oh. Lee. I just really don't know."

The need in her voice drew him. "Listen," he said. The engineer gave him his cue and he nodded in response. "I'm sorry the way things went."

"You are?"

"Sure. What'd you think?"

"It's about time, that's all I can say."

There was a click. "You missed your cue," Merri said.

"Don't cut her off! I know, okay. Give her back to me." Another click. "Shell?"

"If you're too busy with your fans, say so."

"I'm not the kind of guy who'd try to hurt you. Don't you know that?"

"All right," she said. "I'll tell you why I called. I guess you've got a right to know. As of tonight, you don't have anything to worry about."

He nodded again to the engineer, then turned away from the glass. "What's that supposed to mean?"

"What I said."

"I have no idea what you're talking about. I hope."

"You don't have anything to worry about. All right?"

"Listen, just a second, okay? Merri, if you're on the line,

get off." Maybe he heard a click. "Shell, how could you even think of calling the sheriff?"

"On a nice guy like you."

"Okay. Right." He was willing to live and let live. Not women though. They had a sixth sense. Whatever it was you couldn't give, that's what they wanted. Maybe they couldn't help themselves. "I thought we had something pretty nice going for us."

"That's all you can think about—saving your ass."

"Why is it you want to make trouble? You want me to lose my job?"

She sniffed. "You are so sonuvabitching selfish!"

"*I* am? Shelley we were living together, almost. It's not like I'm going to run out on you, anything happens."

"Nothing's going to happen, Lee. I got my period, all right?"

"Oh. Okay."

"But you weren't even thinking about that, right?"

"I knew you weren't pregnant. I told you."

"You *knew*?" She laughed. "Well, you happy now?"

"It's what you wanted too, isn't it?"

Jim and Peg had run out of ways to prepare steak. Jim kept clearing his throat.

"How do you know what I want or don't want?"

"Cue," Merri said, and was gone.

"I mean," Lee said, "if anything had gone wrong, I'd have stuck by you."

"Stuck by me?"

He pictured her on the mattress, redeye in hand, snuggling with the mutt, and imagined the heat of her against him. Asleep, she always had an arm or leg thrown over him, holding him in place.

"What's that supposed to mean, Lee?"

Of course, any fool knew she was bound to get fleas, end up a drunk, and get knocked-up to boot, but you couldn't tell her anything for her own good. Like get yourself a diaphragm. "Listen," he said. At the edge of his vision he saw the engineer wave at the window. "You know how I feel about you."

"Do I?"

"I told you. So what—you want me to prove it?"

"Right," she said.

"Okay, fine. Tell me how and I will. Wait a minute, okay? I have to put you on hold."

"One minute."

"Hey," he said, throaty and jovial, "we can't give you all night together. Not yet anyway." Jim and Peg laughed, plainly relieved to have him back. The weight of thinking up all those words! Everybody out there waiting to hear what you might say, and the second you stopped talking, the silence iced you over. "So here's your big moment, Jim. Ta-ta-ta! Who's to be the lucky lady?"

"Gee, I don't know."

"Cindy, Faye, or Peg?"

"Kinda hard, you know."

"You can't have all three." The time was ripe for Lee to poke a little fun; the listeners loved it and the callers were good sports and laughed at themselves—what else could they do?—but his heart wasn't in it. Just take your pick, Jimbo. Make Peg the steak or take Cindy bowling or have Faye fix a jelly sandwich for your lunch box nights when you head out into the field of security.

"Time's up," Shelley said.

"Don't hang up." He turned back to the mike. "Come on, Jim."

"Gee, I guess, I guess, Peg."

"Okay, Jim! Hear that, Peg?" Lee could have predicted it. Old Jimbo went for the X. How did Peg like it, rare? Jesus, he felt like walking out and letting the whole thing fall apart. "Sorry about that Cindy and Faye—but hey, try us again. We're here every Friday night. All Alone and Blue. In the heart of Ohio." He plugged in one of the dee-jay's music carousels. "Shelley? I'm free. Where were we?"

"You know."

What did she want from him? She'd have him driving a pick-up and square dancing, slapping her around, turning out one kid after another. Merri's light was blinking. The engineer made motions at the glass as though trying to slit his throat with an index finger.

"I'm hanging up," Shelley said.

"Wait."

"For what?"

"Just let's not spoil things, okay?" He waited for her to say something. The silence felt like snow falling. "Listen," he said. His voice sounded distant, as if he were hearing himself on tape delay. "Hey, Shell. If your love life were made into a movie, how do you think it'd be rated?"

"What? I'm on the air?"

"No. You want to go on? I'll take you on, that's what you want."

"I don't need this bullshit."

"Shell?" Her light was off. Marry her? He didn't even know who she was. Tramp teacher, redneck Jew, horny and hard-to-get—Christ, she was a walking contradiction! And it scared him silly to think that might be why he was stuck on her. He hung up, then leaned forward to bang his forehead hard on the edge of table. This old boy is twenty-eight years of age. He hit it again. Time somebody knocked some sense into him.

The engineer rapped on the glass.

Lee stood up and walked out of the booth. "Okay," he said, "*you* think of what to say."

The burning wick of the oil lamp made a whisper like mosquito wings, or his breathing in her hair. Its light, buttery and warm, seemed to soften all it touched. Shelley wrapped her robe about her, its terry cloth rough on her bare skin. She stood backed up to the space heater, her legs so hot she smelled the hair beginning to singe.

When she heard the car turn onto the gravel, she knew it was his. It skidded to a stop, spraying stones. His fist banged on her back door.

"What do you want?" she called. "As if I didn't know."

"Let me in."

The knob rattled, and the door shook in its frame. Sassy growled. Shelley patted the dog's head, "You hush."

"It's cold out here."

"Jump up and down, son."

"What's the matter with you anyway?"

"Why should there be anything the matter with me?" She stared at the locked door, scared that she was seeing the rest of her life. Why didn't he just kick it in? "I'm supposed to fall all over myself now, right? All the women runnin after dreamy Lee Peoples and he picks goofy Shelley. Lucky her!"

"I just now walked out on my job because of you, you know that? And my lease is run out, right? Whose idea was it, my moving?"

She winced at the tinny note of complaint in his voice. Why was she always comforting him for something *he'd* done? Time after time he could say no to her—no plans, no promises, no kids—and that was supposed to be just fine, but she couldn't say it, oh no! If she said no, everything was ruined. "Poor baby," she said.

"Shelley, are you going to let me in or not?"

"Give me ten good reasons."

"I won't try anything."

"Or one."

After a time, he said, "Okay. Just let me get my things there, okay?"

"There's nothing here anymore belongs to you."

"Goddamnit!" The cardboard tacked to the door flew away and his hand came through the hole. Sassy leaped at the door, growling and snapping. Lee let out a yelp.

Shelley smacked Sassy on the ear. "Lay down! Stay!" She jerked open the door. "Get on in here."

"Crazy bitch." He was standing clear of the porch, his face pale and hands cupped together. "Chain her up."

"She won't hurt you."

"She about tore my hand off."

Shelley looked for the leash, gave up and used her robe cord to tie Sassy to a pipe under the kitchen sink. She held the robe pulled together at the waist and sat on the couch. "It's safe now, Mister Peoples."

He stepped in, hesitantly, as if somehow it might be a trap. "Look." He held out his right hand. Blood showed on the knuckles. "She bit me."

"Oh, she doesn't bite." She took his hand in hers. "Those're just scratches. I keep meaning to trim her nails." Shelley shrugged. "You could use a band-aid, but I'm all out."

"I'd settle for a beer."

"Out of that too."

Smiling, he said he'd believe that when he'd seen it.

"No band-aids, no beer," she said flatly. "No diaphragm."

"Okay, listen." He took back his hand and sat beside her. "About us. Let's just give it some time, okay? Together, I mean."

"That a proposal?" She hooted with laughter. "I love it!" He put an arm along the back of the couch. That was Todd's trick, that orangutan!, getting her to where she couldn't think straight. His arm lay there, a dead weight. She twitched her shoulders, and felt it slip away. "Shit," she said, "you mind better that my doggy."

"Shell, look at me."

She turned toward him, her blood pumping so hard she felt her face must be lit up like a stop light. It was right on the tip of her tongue then to tell him the truth. She needed him there because she felt scared sick. All right, she'd lied about her period, but that was only because she had wanted to call him and say something that might make him happy to be with her again.

"Are you just trying to mess up my life?" he asked.

She took in the clear blue eyes, so hopeful, the sandy brows lifted in doubt, and the slight boyish grin ready to grow or fade, a sign of his nervousness, she thought, at having said something so serious. She couldn't tell him now. He wouldn't understand. He had no idea how it felt to break your ass trying to please and all the time knowing that it wasn't good enough and that you had to think yourself lucky to get what little attention you did. Lee was so *pretty*, he just naturally believed he deserved a free ride. She got to her feet, only a little unsteady. Her robe fell open and she left it that way. He'd seen all there was to see. "You know, I think you're right. I guess all I really wanted was to screw you up good."

He said, "Excuse me."

In the cramped bathroom Lee held his hand under the hot tap, then poured Listerine over the shallow cuts. A red blouse and pair of flesh-toned pantyhose dangled from hangers on the shower rod. He leaned over the sink and took slow, deep breaths. The little oval mirror made him think of a porthole.

All those nights he'd laid in his bed in a dormer room under a flat tin roof listening to his folks blaming each other, the sing-song of injured angry voices going on and on as he'd whispered his promise or prayer: Not me, never, not on your life.

How in the world had he got tricked into *needing* her so?

He stepped into the other room. "Shell, I don't know what to say anymore."

"Well, don't look to me. I'm not your Mama."

"Just tell me what you want from me!"

She stared at him. "You wanna go? Your things are by the fridge."

"I give up," he sighed.

"I figured."

In the kitchen he stepped wide of the dog, now eagerly wagging its tail, his friend, and stopped at the stacked boxes. The thought of loading his things into his car and driving anywhere made him groggy, his arms and legs so heavy they felt waterlogged. He glanced at Shelley. Her face was a slate of questions. He took his telescope from the top box, blood trickling down his fingers. "I don't want any of this other stuff."

"Take it all, I'm cramped for space."

"Pitch it." Turning, he opened the scope and lifted it to one eye, wrong way around so it made her appear to be at a safe distance from him. Her figure looked small and glassy, like the pin-up in the barney knob in his Daddy's old Harvester halfton. The telescope flew from his hand, and smacked flat against the refrigerator.

"Nobody gave you the right to look at people here," Shelley said.

Lee touched fingers to his eyelid. The telescope lay in the dog's water dish. "You little bitch!"

"Jew bitch, don't you mean?"

"If you say so, right."

"Ha *ha!*" Her slant grin was bitter with confirmation. "And you'd know, wouldn't you? You redneck prick!"

Her face whipped sideways then and she stumbled back a step as Lee stopped his arm on its backhand swing. He cupped his good hand over the scratched, stinging knuckles of his right. Blood brightened Shelley's lips. His, he thought. She licked them clean. Tears made her eyes look as bright as they had when she'd sat in the audience and he'd slip private little jokes to her from the onstage mike.

"Oh, Lee," Shelley sighed, and folded in against him.

His arms, automatically it seemed, came up to curl about her shoulders. Her softness surprised him. He felt a fluttering in his chest. "Listen," he said, then kissed her on the lips, not tasting blood, and held it for a long time as if either the kiss or the time might make something clear to him. Out of breath, he pulled back. "All I want's what's best for us. Really."

"I just want us to be happy, Lee."

The dog whined, wanting loose.

She lay her head on his chest. "I can hear your heart," she said, and then, "Let's stick together, whatever, all right?"

He listened to the dry ticking of the antique clock, the little seconds joining together, getting big, and then she tilted her face up to his and he remembered it was his turn to say something, and he guessed he'd say yes.

ROBERT FOX

Despite his 1943 origins in New York, Robert Fox has become an Ohio hub. As writer-in-residence and literature coordinator for the Ohio Arts Council, as editor-publisher of Carpenter Press, as reviewer and chronicler of small presses, as teacher at Ohio University and in the Ohio writers-in-the-schools programs, as reader and book editor for Ohio University Press, and as consultant on numerous arts and awards committees . . . he makes things go in Ohio. Bob is also an excellent blues guitarist and piano player . . . and, thankfully, Robert Fox is a fine poet and dedicated fiction writer.

On his farm in Pomeroy, Ohio, he can be found working the fields for new crops or new writing. In his Ohio Arts Council office in Columbus he makes connections for Ohio writers and teachers in an all out campaign for literacy and literature.

Fox declares such a motive for his work in one of the numerous OAC collections of student writing he has edited, "If we are a nation of quasi-literates, as Jonathan Baumbach says, we are in deep trouble. If we have forgotten how to read analytically and creatively, then we have lost the ability to think and react as proud, independent individuals." Voicing his faith in this country's small presses as "the source of most of our current serious poetry and fiction," he warns of the dangers of writing and publishing as big business, that "In this country, the denial of an audience is also a form of censorship, the effects of which can be disastrous for our writers, and subsequently for the nation's literature."

This is the dedicated public figure of Fox; his private visions can be found powerfully expressed in his writing.

The term "magical realism" has become a watchword for such contemporaries as Italo Calvino, Gabriel Garcia Marquez, Julio Cortazar, Octavio Paz, and it is a necessary term for such writing that combines a tradition of realistic and naturalistic fiction with an equally vital tradition of the fantastic. Thus the verifiable detail of realism is enlarged by the magical effects achieved through myth, folktale, and tall tale . . . all through the spell of narrative. Robert Fox's writing is squarely in the tradition of "magical realism," most of it borne out of a kind of meditative, home-grown wonder engendered from his life in the hills of Ohio. Marian Blue describes Fox's narratives: "It transcends limitations, particularly in regards to elements of the fable and short story. In DESTINY NEWS, a number of Fox's brief works exhibit the complexities of the short story . . . within the magical realism tradition. . . . Such blendings and fabulations are artists' natural desires to have their work represent a world as broadly as they would have it." In this desire to have the world be and mean more Fox reveals a basic reforming motivation for his work. Transformation is part of the process he would engender through both immediacy and imaginative possibility.

Commenting on the haunting nature of his writing, Martin Lich clarifies that "His stories are not thrilling in the adventuresome, blood and lust sense. They are thrilling because they embody common emotions in a hauntingly real artistic framework." They have the staying power of all too vivid dreams. Daniel Lusk also notes the sardonic, "eat-it-anyway" quality of his humor: "DESTINY NEWS was written I think by a cynic, whose humor is all that is left of what used to pass for romanticism. By a poet with a compulsion to tell the truth, unless a fable might be more interesting."

Our story, "Frito and the Strong Man," is the last in a series of Frito stories in which the character like our author both inhabits and creates his world.

AWARDS

Ohioana Library Citation in Literature
1987 PEN Syndicated Fiction Project Award

Stories Selected for Anthologies:
SUDDEN FICTION: THE AMERICAN SHORT STORY
A READER OF NEW AMERICAN FICTION
SHORT STORIES FROM THE LITERARY MAGAZINES
CURRENTS: CONCERNS AND COMPOSITION

BOOKS

—Short Stories—
DESTINY NEWS (December Press, 1977)

—Novels—
TLAR & CODPOL, TWO NOVELS: THE LAST AMERICAN REVOLUTION AND CONFESSIONS OF A DEAD POLITICIAN (December Press, 1987)

ROBERT FOX

FRITO AND THE STRONG MAN

Frito had known Edward Strong for years, long before a freak but perhaps inevitable accident paralyzed the man from the waist down. Edward had been the strongest man around the country, lifting tractors off the ground by the front end and bouncing troublemakers out of bars for a living. Now he was causing trouble in bars, wheeling himself in, waving a .22 pistol, accusing this one or that one of messing around with his wife or chasing after his daughter who was too young for men no matter how old she looked. Frito gave no thought to Strong during his entanglement with Lotte, but he had heard that Strong and Jimmy Crown had taken to roaming the countryside together, and something about their companionship kept one out of the hospital and the other out of jail.

After Frito's ill-fated affair with Lotte, he took new notice of his cat Shanti and his dog Nagual. "I named you critters," he said. "I ought to remember why." He decided to meditate again, and was surprised at the ease with which he was once again able to do yoga, and then focus on the spot above and between his eyes that eased him towards eternal peace. It was more of a realm of busy thought than tranquility, for the internal monologue continued, yet it calmed him, bringing him beyond his material concerns. Suddenly he realized it was at least two years since he'd read a book, and immediately he was back in the material world—someone hadn't returned his mother's book on vitamin deficiencies, someone else hadn't returned his $7/16$ths and $3/8$ths sockets which he needed. . . . He knew he must start reading again, something other than body health, if the meditation was to be successful. The control he had hoped to achieve over the world of sense objects was not the reality it once seemed. Books—the world of thought, would help once again toward pure meditation, towards power over the world of circumstance.

Despite his good intentions, he didn't continue the meditation. It was partly the failure to find the right book, when there were so many more immediate (though trivial, he admitted) concerns, and his sprained ankle and pulled thigh muscle in his left leg made it impossible to get into lotus position for a while.

He sprained his ankle naked on the lawn in the morning fog doing a sailor's hornpipe for Shanti and Nagual, who had regarded him strangely when he emerged nude from the house after his bath, having forgotten his change of clothes in the studio. The odd look the two animals gave him demanded a response, and he thought he did a pretty good hornpipe, until his foot came down in a hole and he was suddenly on his back looking up at the fine, swirling mist.

Frito began to collect junked cars. He lined them up in the field along the road, and he had a car and truck in the yard in front of the studio, torn down. He would get them both to run. His collection of wrecks drew an assortment of local scroungers like flies, among them Edward Strong and his sidekick, Jimmy crown.

Frito began collecting the cars when he traded the couch Peter and Mary had given him for a 1960 pickup truck that did not run. Peter and Mary were not their real names—they had changed them after becoming Christians. Though they had finally given up trying to convert Frito, he did not trust them. They returned from a failed mission in South America where they were almost shot as spies, and offered Frito the couch, which was in good shape, a pleasant addition to the old house, but he was uncomfortable with it, thinking if he fell asleep on it, he'd dream about the Gospels. So he traded it for the truck. Acquisition of the truck led to other vehicles, many with interchangeable parts, and when the word got out that Frito traded or sold parts, Jimmy and Edward appeared.

"We're just on the way to the carry-out," Jimmy said, and offered Frito the last generic beer, warm from the floor of the car.

Frito refused. He never liked beer, particularly warm beer, in the middle of the day.

"Oh, come on, buddy," Jimmy said as if his feelings were hurt. He and Edward balanced open cans on their laps.

"I'll take that old weed any day over a beer," Frito said.

"Well get in the car, buddy," Jimmy said. "We know where there's plenty."

"Got all I need," Frito said.

Jimmy got out of the car, bent and stiff like an old man, sat down on the hood, and rolled a cigarette. "Been a long time there, pardner."

"It has," Frito said. "Where've you guys been hiding out?"

"I mean since you fooled with cars. You sticking transistors in them again?"

"Naw," Frito said. "Just trying to make them run."

As a mechanic, Jimmy Crown had flashes of brilliance that equaled his brother-in-law, Raynor Shine, but he didn't have Raynor's discipline. Not to say that Raynor didn't drink, but Raynor didn't cry how the world mistreated him, or step out of houses without porches, thinking porches were there, and break his leg. Despite Jimmy's inability to work at a regular job, he was drawn to cars in the same way artists and preachers know their callings. Now that Jimmy's old buddy Daryl Westlake was gone for good, living near his divorced wife in Florida so he could be near his kids, Jimmy had taken on the paralyzed Edward Strong as his partner, to ride about the country, tinkering with cars to make enough money to buy gas and keep them in beer.

Unlike Jimmy and Daryl who complained how they were mistreated, Edward directed his great anger outward. If Jimmy was low or hurting, in Edward's mind, there was a reason: a person who'd done him wrong, and Edward thought they should get him. Jimmy, who never harmed anyone in his life, except his wife and children, was continually talking Strong out of one vengeful act or another.

The real reason Jimmy and Edward made this first visit was to borrow Frito's 3/4 inch sockets. You have to know how Frito is about tools. He will take on with a plumber or carpenter friend for a few days or a few weeks to earn enough money for particular tools. Or, he will buy equipment to spend twenty-four hours a day making plastic flower pots to sell to the mothers of university students at a flea market in Carthage, which in turn will give him the cash to spend on tolls. Then he will spend days in Carthage, trying to catch up with the Snap-On truck on its rounds. He will drive to Carthage earlier than he normally rises, eat a huge breakfast at Perkins Pancakes, wiring himself with coffee, and wait for the Snap-On truck at different garages until it finally appears. The Snap-On man is never at his appointed rounds, but eventually does appear, or Frito flags him down at the side of the road, and buys a set of screwdrivers with ebony handles and perfect silky vanadium steel stems that make it look like it should sit on a blue velvet turntable under a spotlight at the Museum of Modern Art.

If you saw Jimmy Crown and Edward Strong, you would not want to lend them anything, let alone tools which could be confused with artworks. If you saw them get out of the huge Oldsmobile with the 440 motor, buy cheap beer and then stop at the old woman's store with the lone pump in Pondville and put fifty cents worth of gas in the tank, which might or might not be enough to get them home, you would not trust them with a dimestore pocket-knife. But Frito did. And they always returned his tools when they said they would.

"Here you are, buddy," Jimmy said, returning a wrench. His face was striped with grease, like warpaint, his tee shirt stained a dark green, and, though his fist was dirty, the tool would be about as clean as when it was borrowed.

And now that Frito was in the junk business, working on the two wrecks in his yard, Jimmy and Edward had the opportunity to repay him. If Jimmy had trouble diagnosing a problem or getting a part to fit, Edward insisted on being lifted up onto the hood, or if Jimmy was under the vehicle, Edward would get out of the car, into the wheelchair, out of the wheelchair, and pull himself under too, and with still powerful arms, push Jimmy out of the way. "That old drunk ain't strong enough to hold a nut while he turns a bolt." A saying he often repeated before Jimmy even stepped out of the car to attempt a repair.

They had access to numerous wrecks about the entire county, and if Frito needed a part he didn't have, they usually knew where to locate it. If they needed parts out of Frito's storehouse, they brought appropriate exchanges.

Frito first met Edward Strong years before, when Brian Stevens took him to the old Schoolhouse Playground, which sat between the boarded up brick building and the Schoolhouse Cemetery. "You won't believe what you are about to see," Brian said. They had just come from Jimmy's muddy ravine of a front yard littered with cars pitched on their sides or completely overturned. Wilma said the men were at the Schoolhouse Playground, and when they arrived, they could see, between the tile building and parked cars, and the headstones from the cemetery, the men standing around a rusted Farmall tractor without front wheels, drinking beer. Brian didn't have to point out Strong. He was the shortest man there, and Frito did not believe he was going to do anything unusual until he saw the man's hand and forearms. Then he remembered the strongman show he had seen as a boy on the boardwalk of Coney Island: the Mighty Atom, with flowing black hair and a Rabbinical beard, the short man with the huge hands and forearms who broke nails in his teeth, twisted horseshoes, sliced bricks in half with karate-like chops. . . .

The men talked aimlessly and drank their beer and then Daryl Westlake insisted that the tractor wasn't that heavy and that anyone who knew what they were doing could lift it, because when he was logging in New Brunswick, he had lifted logs three or four times as heavy as the tractor. Daryl was serious and not very drunk, so the men leaning against the Farmall pushed themselves off like swimmers in slow motion and Daryl planted his feet in front of the machine, grabbed the frame and began straining. Then he eased off and turned to the men. "Just warming up a bit here," his face dark with blood. He spit on his palms, rubbed his hands together, crouched, grabbed the frame and strained once again, the tendons standing out taut in his neck, reaching to his shoulders. Then he cried out, let go of the tractor, and doubled over in the mud.

"His back," Jimmy shouted. "He done broke his back!"

"No, it's my leg," Daryl said, clutching his thigh.

Soon Daryl was back on his feet, limping around in circles. Then Edward Strong looked among the men to see if anyone else wanted to try. He did not dare, or ask, or smirk. No one moved. He walked up to the tractor, planted his feet squarely, crouched, took several deep breaths, and began to lift. He stood before the machine, gritting his teeth, looking not unlike Daryl, but then the front end rose slowly out of the mud. He held the tractor in the air so that the men could measure the distance, and then set it back and collected his money in silence.

Frito didn't know how many tractors or cars or whatever Strong lifted about the countryside, and he assumed that Strong's paralysis resulted from an attempted lift, but didn't know for sure. Strong was no longer always victorious in fights, and it was possible too that a car wreck was the cause of his paralysis and downfall.

Frito wondered how Strong felt about being Jimmy's Crown's sidekick, if Strong even thought anything about it or just lived mechanically, going along with Jimmy because it was something to do. They had been driving about the country now for some time and it kept Strong out of trouble. Frito became so sure of the quality of Jimmy's influence, that when Jimmy fell to pieces again from too much cheap beer and not enough decent food and was in the hospital again to get dried out and beefed up, he was sure Edward would get into trouble again.

In fact, both Sparky Olson and Shorty Briggs told him Strong was going to get into trouble. It was a fact. So, Frito decided to visit Strong to find out for himself.

Strong lived in a trailer on Coon Pen Ridge with his wife and daughter. It had been a nice home once, a clearing in a grove of trees, but now two cars sat with their hubs half-submerged in mud and various other kinds of trash lying about in what had once been a neat yard. The trailer itself needed paint. The aluminum paneling around the base was breaking apart, peeling away, and the porch, which Strong had added on, also needed repair. Strong's wife tried to keep up the appearance somewhat, with macrame planters. Great viney plants swarmed out of hangars, about the pots, enclosing the porch like a jungle, and there were additional plants lining all the windows.

When Frito drove up, Edward Strong was sitting in the front yard in his wheelchair. Frito did a double take, thinking the man in the chair was not Strong at all, but some relative perhaps, a Nam vet, for the man in the chair had a beard. Edward's once brown hair was a dark iron grey now, and his beard came in pure white. It made his blue eyes even more piercing.

Frito extended a hand and Edward withdrew his from under the blanket on his lap, but instead of a handshake, Frito found himself looking down the barrel of a revolver. His hands automatically rose.

"Oh," Strong mumbled and put the gun down. "Didn't mean to scare you," he said, nonchalant. "I just have some business to take care of."

"That kind of business is going to get somebody hurt and you in jail," Frito said. He looked about the yard. Someone had dug up a patch of ground in front of the trailer and planted petunias. A swath of earth in the yard was also overturned and a row of six tomato plants stood tied to stakes. A coon had also gotten into a plastic garbage bag, and milk cartons and beer cans were neatly laid out.

"You've been up here a long time," Frito said.

"Ten years," Strong said.

"I came by once with Brian Stevens and Jimmy Crown right after you settled in," Frito said.

"I was managing the Road Hog Tavern then," Strong said. "Made pretty good money. It was a good, clean place. Never had no trouble there while I was running it. Was a man then. Now I'm only half."

Frito almost reflexively said something about mental attitude. On TV he had seen all the happy parapalygics who overcame great odds to create successful lives, careers, continue successful marriages.

"What kind of business you expecting?" Frito asked. He thought he might as well get down to the heart of the matter.

"There's people goin round saying a lot of things," Strong said. "People didn't use to talk like that before I was a cripple. There's people try to take advantage of my wife, you know. Well, it's time I got things straightened out a bit, levelled off. I can still stand on my own two feet, if you know what I mean."

"Why don't you come down to the hospital with me, visit Jimmy?"

Strong broke out in a big grin. "You visiting that old drunk in the hospital? You're crazy, wasting your time like that. Ain't you got nothin' better to do? He ever gets out of the hospital he'll come back around here." Strong wheeled his chair around sharply so that he was sitting with his back facing Frito. He sat like that for some time while Frito tried to think of a next move, a next word that would not rouse Strong's mercurial temper.

"Follow me," Strong said over his shoulder, and wheeled his chair onto a path that led behind the trailer, towards the woods. "Just want to show you something back here."

The explanation didn't lessen Frito's anxiety. He hoped that the path could be seen from the road, but it was blocked by the trailer. He followed Strong, who wheeled his chair quickly, but took care across planks laid down across wet spots. At the treeline, Frito saw a table and several chairs.

It was an old wooden kitchen table with the legs cut down a few inches to make it a perfect height for Strong, who wheeled himself to one side of the table and motioned for Frito to sit down opposite. When Frito was seated, Strong placed his right arm on the table, pivoting on his elbow, opening and closing his hand as if bidding welcome.

"Come on," Strong said.

"Arm wrestle you? Are you kidding?"

"You chicken?"

"No, I . . ."

"You think you can beat me now that I'm . . ."

"Just the opposite. . . . I don't have a prayer against you."

Strong heaved a hearty laugh. "You don't look like a weakling. I seen you build that building, chop wood, haul hay. You don't look like a weakling to me. Now come on."

"Okay," Frito said and got his arm into position. He didn't have time to think about it. The moment Strong's hand took his he knew it was over. He wasn't prepared for the sudden authority of Strong's grip that overtook him like an undertow and brought him down.

"What d'you mean," Strong said. His nostrils flared. His blue eyes pierced. "You tryin to humor me?"

"No I . . . I wasn't ready," Frito said.

"Wasn't ready," Strong mimicked. "Well, we'll try again." He put his arm on the table. Frito followed suit but held up his other hand in a wait sign.

"I've got to think about this a second," he said.

Strong smiled. "Think all you want. Now let's go."

Frito still held his other hand in the wait sign while he studied the table, looking to see if it was level or if there were any advantages.

"You want to switch sides?" Strong said. "Pick whatever side you want."

"No," Frito said. "I'm ready as I'll ever be." He placed his elbow in the exact location he wanted and took a deep breath. He looked at Strong to say okay and then received the rough, unwanted embrace of Strong's hand. Frito exerted a sudden push that caught Strong off guard. He was actually pushing Strong's hand down. He knew he had the edge and if he could give it all he had he might win. Just as he exerted every last bit of pressure he could muster, Strong suddenly realized what was happening and Frito felt as if he were pushing the wall of a building. Though Frito had the advantage, he couldn't move Strong's hand down.

Slowly, Strong began to come back, inching Frito upward. Frito fought, his arm, body quivering.

"Don't quit or I'll kill you," Strong said between his teeth.

Frito said nothing but directed another thrust against Strong's arm, Strong's wrist quivering momentarily but it became solid again. He waited until Frito could push no more, held him deadlocked at the starting point, Frito afraid for his life to quit, even if his arm fell off, right at the shoulder, he'd leave it there, deadlocked with Strong through the sunset into the night, and he'd go home, go to sleep. He didn't need the arm anyway. It would be useless for weeks now.

Frito arrived at some spiritual place far away from the match yet his arm kept wrestling on its own, finding an outside source of strength until Strong began to get bored and brought Frito down.

"I told you I didn't think you was weak."

Frito lifted his right arm in his left hand, examining it, squeezing it.

"There's not too many people could beat you," Strong said. "Those long arms you got give you an edge. You ought to hang out at the Road Hog awhile. Make you some extra change."

Frito massaged his forearm, flexed his wrist, and then let it alone. He looked about the yard, the treeline. "This is a nice location." He could smell the breath of the woods. Birds echoed high in trees. "You picnic over here?"

"It's where I meditate," Strong said.

Even though Frito was seated, the words made him feel as if he'd fallen into the chair. But the chair itself, a simple old wooden kitchen chair with the yellow paint peeling and the exposed grain weathered gray . . . the chair itself began to vibrate and shake as if it were in the midst of a struggle between time and space for supremacy. Frito stared at Strong to reassure himself it was the same man. The white beard, the wide nostrils, blue eyes, thick lips. It was Strong, all right. As far as he could tell, no demon had come from the woods and replaced him. "How do you meditate?"

"I sit right where I'm sitting now. This exact spot. Then I think about things. What I was before. What I am now. About my wife. My little girl who's almost all growed up now. I think about what they do, who they run around with, what it all means, what good any of it does."

Frito felt a new warmth, an unexpected kinship with Strong. Instead of a demon, Strong was actually a good spirit, come to get him back on the track of meditation. He knew there was hope for everyone to overcome the oppressive, debilitating circumstances of their lives—to *transecnd!* "What *does* it all mean?" he asked Strong, excited.

"It don't mean *shit,*" Strong said. "That's what I conclude. All my life I live like an animal, doin' this, doin' that, without thinking about it. Sometimes it works out, sometimes it don't. Sometimes I feel good, real good. Sometimes I get hurt. Now I get a chance to think about it and the only difference is—I think about it. Only difference between us and possums is we think about it. We bullshit a lot about what we do but it don't make a difference in what we do. Don't make us different. If a possum wants to bite the head off a chicken, he goes ahead and does it. He don't stand around and say to the world, 'Jesus says in the Bible, blah-blah-blah,' or 'That hen's been hangin around with that Communist rooster from Cuba or Poland blah-blah-blah.' "

"But where do you go from the bullshit?" Frito asked.

"Ain't no place *to* go. Can't go no place without legs. I think of a few scores I could even, but that wouldn't do no good."

"The meditation—it helps things make sense . . ."

Strong interrupted him with an angry denial. "I just finished saying it don't make sense."

"I thought you said that when you think about it, you see that violence isn't going to solve anything."

"It'll get rid of certain trouble makers!" Strong brandished the pistol.

Frito knew he should change the subject but he felt compelled to ask the next question, despite the risk. "Are there particular people you blame for what happened to your legs?"

"Yeah, me," he said. "My damn fault for acting like a damn fool. And even so, it ain't fair."

Numerous questions and answers about fairness and responsibility flashed through Frito's mind in the brief silence that followed. Then he stood up and stretched and noticed for the first time the row of young marijuana plants in cutaway plastic jugs that sat along the tree line.

"I though that'd be the first thing you'd a noticed," Strong said. "Man's got to make a living somehow—can't be dependent on his women for every cent. You can see how much is here and it ain't much. But you'd be surprised how many's out there would like to take the little bit I got. Take it away from me. But they ain't gonna. That's all I can say."

"I just wanted to ask you another question," Frito said. "Before, you mentioned something about sitting in that exact spot when you meditate. Does it make you feel stronger there—more in control or something—as opposed to where I was sitting?"

Strong eyed him strangely.

"I read a book once that said you could have more power in certain places where you feel comfortable—more than comfortable, feel right."

"I sit here, I sit there, I wheel down the row this way or up there or into the woods. Come on, buddy, all this talk got my mouth too dry. There's some cold beer inside."

Frito did not visit Jimmy Crown in the hospital. He would have driven Edward in if he were willing to go, but Strong thought the idea was ridiculous. Frito was not about to waste his time, as Brian Stevens did, years ago, bringing Jimmy new car magazines which were left in the hospital, and hear Jimmy tell Wilma how he'd never rise from the bed, how he'd taken his last ride. Frito had accompanied the entire crew once, and the memory was still vivid: Wilma, who had left Jimmy years ago, needing to be coaxed into the hospital because she was barefoot, and Daryl Westlake cutting up in front of the nurses aides, looking at himself in the mirror over the sink, slapping his thigh and crying out. "Ain't that a handsome son-of-a-bitch!"

Now Jimmy had no one to cry to, Frito thought, and he'd be out soon, hunting up the first beer he could get his hands on.

Frito thought of visiting Strong again, of even getting Strong into his truck, the two of them wandering about the countryside. He wanted to learn more about Strong's "meditation." Perhaps in some way they could help each other. Frito thought that if he could start meditating again on his own he could tell Strong about what he was doing, and maybe get Strong headed toward some form of transcendence.

Of course, Frito himself was far from transcendence at the moment, with the two wrecks on his lawn, hoods off, crazy monsters waiting to devour more time, money, good energy. Ten years before, while married to Rhonda, goofing off on drugs most of the time, the only clear-mindedness he had was directed towards cars. And that wasn't very clear. Though he hardly smoked at all now, he seemed to have reverted again, to that apparently fruitless business of repairing a motor vehicle for the hell of repairing it, since it wasn't going to transport you anyplace different from where you already were.

Frito needed to asses his ego, which he had once thought he had succeeded in merging with the flow of reality. He couldn't identify the cause of his trouble as his ego, but felt it must be the ego, lurking undetected, like a disease learned to become immune. If he could muster the discipline to meditate, he could sort it all out, check on the ego, do good for his fellow man, in a far better way than by loaning tools.

He knew he had once been regarded as a guru of sorts, a man of virtue. But whatever illumination he had radiated was lost. He couldn't be far from it, though, and his visit with Edward Strong had provided him with a challenge, just the incentive he needed to sort out the priorities in his life.

He was fascinated by Strong's character. Before the visit, he had thought that Strong's fierce anger was buffered by Jimmy Crown's buffoonery. Now he was convinced it was Strong's own meditations, whose effectiveness Strong denied, that kept him intact, able to deal with an anger multiplied X number of times because of his paralysis. He doesn't even realize how much in control he is, Frito thought.

Frito was in the midst of rebuilding the rear brakes of the truck sitting on his lawn, discovering one spring was bad and that both bleeders were broken off, but it didn't matter because his mind was excited about the challenge of dealing with Strong's complex but barely articulate thought processes. He crawled out from under the truck, thinking of where he would locate these additional parts, whose wreck was available? but not disturbed by these unforeseen obstacles which, a few days before, you have thrown him into a bitter fury. As he came out from under, Sparky Olson drove up.

He and Sparky were once again on speaking terms after their run-in with thieves and crazy women and Sparky didn't mince words. He simply got out of his car and walked up to Frito and said, "Strong's in big trouble. Shot two people last night."

Frito waited to hear more.

"Shot Marvin Koons trying to steal his plants and then shot into his trailer and hit his daughter in the arm. Hadn't been for those plants in the window he would've fractured her clavicle. Some fool had come up with Koons and when Koons was hit he yelled for his buddy to come out, and Edward poured lead into that trailer, not knowing who was inside."

"Anyone hurt real bad?"

"No. Don't look like anyone will press charges, either. Except his wife. She don't need no dangerous drunk like that around. Law's after him and he's hiding out down at the home place if you want to see him. I don't know he's there. Law finds him, well, he knew the house was empty and he just moved in. They may find him, they may let it all die down. You want to kill someone, Briggs County's the place. Ain't got no law."

Frito said nothing, stood staring off across the road into the meadow and so Sparky continued, "I knew Edward'd get in trouble without Jimmy around. He's just that type, you know, broods about things a bit too much, then blames the world for his problems."

"You blame him for shooting a man sneaking onto his place to steal valuable property?"

"I thought you was non-violent," Sparky said. "Thought you told me once attachment to property and all that stuff just confused your life." He said that in a huff, not waiting for a response, and got into his car. "Just thought I'd let you know is all," he called and drove off.

Frito still did not move. While Sparky had chirped out his information, the word "duty" had flashed into his mind—for the first time in over a year. He was trying to ascertain his duty or responsibility when Sparky made the remark about property. Suddenly the subject changed. He had once connected Sparky with the thefts of gas and the battery from his tractor, and though he had dismissed it a long time ago, Sparky's remarks made it all clear now. "If I am attached to property, then he could tell someone what I've got that could be stolen because I won't care—it won't matter! And he even encourages me to say those things, as if he agrees, and quotes from the Bible as if it means something!" Frito said this all out loud. His mind raged. He wished he could have been with Strong to help stop Koons, but also stop Edward from shooting up his own home. He wished he would've had a gun and waited in ambush when the thieves had come into his tractor shed. But none of this violence, in defense of property, made sense either. Sparky was right.

Even if he had meditated to begin the day, he still would not have been prepared for this overload. "I'll do it now, then," he said out loud and gathered up his tools and went inside to draw a bath, rather than wasting the time it would take to go to and from the pond.

That decision, and acting towards it, already began to calm him down and the thought process was well underway so that by the time he was towelled off and then in his shorts and sandals and then on the rug in the one upstairs room in the house he used, for that purpose only—where no one could find him—it was as if he'd never stopped meditating. But he had to slow down—his thoughts were racing, colliding, and he did several exercises he'd reserved for late in the day, giving him control over breath, and, as a result, over time, too. He was now approaching the implacable calm of the spirit, so that when he went to visit Strong, he would have already had a glimpse of peace, and with luck, if Edward was not drunk, Frito's example would be just that—an example that would be irresistible to someone who had already found the path, had begun to move in the right direction on his own.

Frito got out of his truck cautiously, shouting to Strong that it was him, alone, that no one followed. There was no answer. "If it's okay to come in, say so." Frito hesitated behind the front fender, expecting to hear a shot, or see a gun crash through a window. "I'm going to town, Edward," he shouted. "Want to know if you need anything."

Frito heard an incoherent response muffled within and decided to venture out into the open. He started to the front porch and heard, "Back door—in the kitchen," and followed the overgrown path around to the back.

He pushed through the screen door and saw Strong in his wheelchair staring through the window to make sure Frito wasn't being followed. A high-powered rifle leaned up against the wall. Strong wheeled around and faced Frito. Strong was drunk, probably had been for days. His skin was blue, eyes bloodshot, hair and beard matted. Frito could smell his sweat across the room.

"Law wouldn't be following you, would it? I mean without you knowing about it?" Strong's eyes narrowed to slits.

"Sparky and me the only ones know you're here. Not even Sparky's wife."

"Then why the fuck don't you leave me alone?"

"Just came to see if you need anything—like I told you, I'm going to town."

"You come over to bugger me? All prettied up like that? Take advantage of a poor cripple like me?"

Frito was unprepared for that, and now had to add a whole new dimension to understanding Strong's violence.

"You think now I'm crippled, I've queered up—you think . . ."

"I've just been meditating. I haven't in a long time—you know, until you mentioned it the other . . ."

"You makin' fun of me. Come over to make . . ." he trailed off, eyed his gun. "All I fucking do is meditate," he mumbled. "Drink, meditate, and shoot."

"In that order," Frito said.

"You got it, buddy. And while you're all prettied up and in one piece, why don't you go and get yourself some cunt. You ain't going to find no pussy around here."

"That's good advice," Frito said and saluted and turned towards the door.

"Damn right it's damn good advice," Strong shouted after him.

Frito hadn't had any great expectations for his visit, and as he walked back over the path to his truck, he felt calm and relaxed. He knew at the same time that his life was completely in the hands of an irresponsible drunk, who was also not completely sane. It didn't matter. Frito had a sense of detachment, of clarity that hadn't come his way in a long time. If he made it out of there alive, he would spend the rest of the day away from enslavement of various sorts, just visiting friends in Carthage.

He'd forgotten to ask Strong if Jimmy Crown was home from the hospital yet. But that didn't matter either. Frito made it to the truck, got into the cab and started the motor. He looked towards the house, wondering if he'd be able to see the long barrel of the rifle aimed at him. But the windows were mirrors.

He had to maneuver the truck several times to aim towards the road, then picked up speed and descended the hill, not knowing when he would be out of sight or out of range. The gun did have a scope on it.

Once back on the main roads, completely out of immediate danger, Frito lost the sense of buoyancy he had before he'd arrived. Now the challenge and the threat were gone. But he had done whatever it was he had to do, whatever *that* was.

Frito found the parts he needed in the junk pile next to Raynor Shine's garage. He was driving away when Jimmy Crown suddenly appeared and came up to Frito's door. Frito shut the motor off.

Jimmy looked twenty pounds lighter and his skin was now colorless instead of blotchy and bruised.

"When are you and Strong going to drop by?" Frito asked.

"Not for a long, long time, buddy," Jimmy said, giving a deep cough, which he took as a signal to roll a cigarette. "Not for a long, long time."

"You two have a falling out?"

"Hell no," Jimmy said, taking a deep drag on his cigarette. "Law got him. They put him away this time."

"So there is law in Briggs County. You can't get away with shooting people after all."

Jimmy laughed. "Hell no, buddy. Game warden got him. Shot a deer out of season and with an illegal weapon."

"Strong went deer hunting in his wheelchair?"

Jimmy laughed again. "Deer come to him, grazing right outside the window. He didn't even open it. Called Sparky on the phone to come down dress it for him so he'd have some meat to eat and someone overheard on the party line and called the game warden. No sir, he don't have money for bail. Wife won't bail him out."

"The law reasons crazy," Frito said. "It's okay if you shoot people. They figure you got reasons. But you can't be hungry except during deer season."

"Shows you what kind of people makes the laws," Jimmy wheezed, summing up the rationale behind his life, his abdication.

Frito turned the ignition key and as the motor fired Jimmy backed off. "Don't do anything I wouldn't do, buddy," he said, saluting with his cigarette.

"I never was that good," Frito said, and drove home past the lines of wrecked cars that sat in front of tar paper sheds and old trailers inhabited by large families. He knew some of the families—the women protesting how much they loved kids, kids whose skin appeared to be made of bleached tar paper or dirty cloth, kids who put motors on their bicycles as soon as they were able, creating dust clouds on the dirt road, or sliding in the mud in back of their trailers. Sometimes he played with these kids, wrestling with them, having them gang up on him, rolling with them in the dust. Why couldn't he find a woman who liked kids? Time was passing too quickly without a family. It would pass even faster with children, he thought. He could sit in the hammock with a joint, watch them sprout, grow like plants in time-lapse movies.

He was deeply troubled by the news of Strong in jail, angry at himself for not knowing why, and angry at the thought of possibly meditating to get rid of the anger, shake the ego loose again which kept returning like unwanted invisible clothes dressing him everytime he reached nakedness.

I should be glad he's in jail, Frito thought, not be troubled by it. I could easily be on his hit list, even though I did not beat him at arm wrestling. Then it seemed to Frito that jail was the ultimate injustice for Strong, although it was an unexpected real justice in the practical world; it was an affirmation of Strong's worldview, the sum of Strong's version of meditation that led not to clarity and freedom, but to futility. That meditation should lead to imprisonment was paradoxical—the source of his anger, Frito realized—until it suddenly occurred to him that Strong did not meditate—he couldn't possibly have ever meditated; Strong used spiritual language for self-pity. How obvious!

Frito was on the paved state road now, crawling along at the same speed he drove on the rutted township road, passed by one angry vehicle after another, upset so soon into his enlightenment by all the anger around him, washing past him like a tide, filtering so easily into his own consciousness. Why are they angry at me for holding them back? I'm not holding them back because they're passing me! Why the dirty looks? Suppose my truck was crippled—they'd be angry at that too! Or if I was hauling a load of gravel they'd curse me out.

Though Frito now had the parts he'd sought for months and had pictured himself spending the rest of the day beneath the car, coating himself with mud, grease and blood, he decided to take the day off—make it a day of purge, of cleansing. He would bathe, do yoga, then meditate. What if one of his neighbors showed up with a jug of whiskey, a bag of buds? He'd pretend he wasn't home. He would concentrate as hard as he ever had in his life to make himself invisible, convince the unwanted guest that while his vehicles were around, he himself was off in the woods, or in the fields. He was sure an unwanted guest would arrive, spoiling his plans—challenging his resolve, his spiritual strength.

He felt he was riding in a tail wind, passing landmarks to his home faster than he should have. He also felt he was being pursued, driven, and then had the feeling his mother was trying to communicate with him, maybe ask for the return of her vitamin book. He would call her even before he meditated. Maybe something had happened to his Dad. His brother Ted kept accusing him of not keeping in touch, that his Dad often complained of the distance between them.

He came down the road towards his driveway too fast, realize he was home, slammed on the brakes throwing the small truck into a skid, jerked the wheel and gunned the motor. As he wheeled sharply into his driveway, his rear bumper banged on the corner post of the yard fence, splitting a seasoning crack.

He parked and went to inspect the damage and then saw the wasps issuing from the post like a cloud of smoke, heading for the truck, circling to find the perpetrator. Before he started to run, it seemed to him the wasps assumed the shape of a man, hovering in the sky above him, stretching its arms out to him, about to lunge. He did not have the time to exercise the kind of thought control or telepathic communication he used with his honey bees which kept him from ever being stung. Then he was running, the wasps stinging him on the ears, the back of the neck, the fingers, before he shut the door behind them.

He should put ice on the stings, but there were too many of them. A hot bath he thought would draw the poison out. A hot bath, then he would go upstairs to the clean room, the special room, do yoga, and then meditate. He removed his shirt, inspected himself in the bathroom mirror. The stings ached, throbbed in rotation, some disappearing while others took up the beat, an orchestra of pain. He opened the taps wide, let the water pound into the tub.

The phone rang—it was his mother. She'd been trying all morning to reach him. "I had the worst dream about you," she said. "I thought it was stupid—you'll think I'm crazy, but I wanted to make sure you're alive. I dreamt someone you know killed you, over some dope, or maybe they were on dope or something. I know they drink a lot of moonshine where you live and their dope is supposed to be better than . . ."

"I'm okay, Mom," he said. "I'm sorry about the vitamin book. I've been looking for it to send back. It's helped. I got rid of the spots."

"Forget about the book. I wanted to make sure you were all right. I'd tried several times this morning. If I couldn't get you I was going to call Rhonda, see if she'd maybe heard something."

"Rhonda?" he asked, even more confused. "Where is she?" thinking maybe she'd moved back to Ohio without his knowing, was planning to come back to him even though they were divorced. "Where is Rhonda?"

"She's in Brooklyn, isn't she?"

"That's what I thought," Frito said. "How's Dad?" he asked.

The water pounded into the tub. It sounded like another phone was ringing somewhere nearby, but he didn't have another phone. It was the motor of a truck, a pale green truck coming up his driveway past his truck, almost driving up on the front porch.

"The dream was so real, so vivid. I usually don't believe in this kind of psychic . . ."

"But it's real," Frito shouted into the receiver. "I rushed home because I knew you were trying to call me!"

Orrin Shine got out of the truck. He was the youngest of the Shine/Crown clan, also a mechanic, but notorious for his engine rebuilds, installing piston rings in reverse order so that motors burned more oil than before his overhaul, or for not setting valve clearances so that the valves burned up as soon as the motor was back in the car.

Frito did not want Orrin there. He was going to have to will him away, but he was unable to concentrate while on the phone with his mother. Orrin was snooping around, sniffing like a dog, it looked like, to see what he could get into if Frito wasn't there. Frito was sure it was Orrin who walked off with the beautiful half-inch ratchet handle that Brian Stevens had given him years ago, which Brian had stolen while in the Marines. It was Snap-On quality or better, manufacturer unknown. He did not know what else Orrin might have gone off with. He needed to get rid of Orrin now. His mother was talking a blue streak. He wanted to answer her. She was talking a mile a minute. Then Orrin was pressing his face to the window, shielding his eyes from the sun. His blond hair was combed in a neat pompadour. His blue eyes were crossed. His mouth was set in a grin, his lower teeth crooked, his upper teeth newly gone.

How did he lose his teeth? Frito wondered while wishing Orrin gone and no longer hearing his mother with whom he wanted to backtrack, pick up the conversation at some meaningful point.

"Are you all right. Are you sure you're okay? You sound like something's bothering you. Are you still there? I worry about some of those neighbors of yours. They remind me too much of those maniacs in *Deliverance*. I know you have a lot of nice neighbors too. . . ."

What I need is a pack of dogs, Frito thought. A pack would be much better than a mastiff or a blood-red doberman or a crazy dog like Stromboli. A pack of dogs would keep Orrin from ever getting out of his truck. Meanwhile he was waving to Orrin who still had his face pressed to the glass unable to see Frito. "I've got to go, Ma," Frito said, trying to think of what to say to Orrin without seeming rude. Orrin would no doubt have a warm six pack in his truck which he would offer. Suddenly a stream of filthy hot water from the bathroom hit his bare feet where he stood in the kitchen, holding the phone.

JACK MATTHEWS

Jack Matthews is a most Ohio writer, born in Columbus, Ohio, 1925, educated at Ohio State University, since 1964 teacher and sometimes director of the creative writing program at Ohio University, Distinguished Professor since 1978. Six successful novels, five short story collections and two poetry books distinguish his busy career as professor and author. Beyond that he is a critic, reviewer, and author of two books on the art of book collecting.

His sense of location in Ohio is further highlighted by his subject and stance as a contemporary writer, as Stanley W. Lindberg suggests: "Jack Matthews' mature imagination lives in the American heartland where it was shaped. In fact, Matthews is at his best when he is taking the pulse of Middle America (not merely a geographical area, of course, but a state of consciousness extending far beyond Matthews' native Ohio)." Rather than being confined by his Ohio place sense (He lives and works in Athens, Ohio) he speaks for it and through it toward a universal sense of life today.

His writing is rich in its weave of Midwestern history and myth, as in his fine TALES OF THE OHIO LAND, but also in his more contemporary stories. Matthews declares, "All stories are philosophical probes, hypotheses, heuristic journeys, maps of powerful and conceivable realities, speculations, ceremonies of discovery."

Probably Ohio's most prolific fiction writer, he has won this praise from his fellow writers. Tim O'Brien writing in THE NEW YORK TIMES BOOK REVIEW finds his DUBIOUS PERSUASIONS "Filled with the wry and wistful insights of middle age . . . Matthews is a master of prose conversation and deadpan charm," to which Eudora Welty adds that the stories are "Blessed with honesty, clarity, directness, proportion, and a lovely humor." Benjamin DeMott exclaims of THE CHARISMA CAMPAIGNS, "A marvelous short novel" to which Anthony Burgess adds, "This book already has the feel of an American classic." His writing is consistently praised for its sense of language, its humor, and its philosophical insight. Doris Grumbach praises his narrative art in CRAZY WOMEN, thusly, "His heights are towering and intense."

Matthews offers this critical insight to his central themes and his view of fiction, and it seems most appropriate to our story "The Smoke of Invisible Fires" included here: "Man's character is his fate, but he should never let this fact inhibit his real freedom of the real moment. I celebrate this truth in my stories, as well as in the act of writing them."

AWARDS

Guggenheim Fellowship (1974)
Individual Artist Grant from the Ohio Arts Council (various years)

Stories selected for:
THE BEST AMERICAN SHORT STORIES and PRIZE STORIES: THE O. HENRY AWARDS
Ohioana Award

BOOKS

—Novels—
HANGER STOUT, AWAKE! (Harcourt Brace, 1967)
BEYOND THE BRIDGE (Harcourt Brace, 1970)
THE TALE OF ASA BEAN (Harcourt Brace, 1971)
THE CHARISMA CAMPAIGNS (Harcourt Brace, 1972)

PICTURES OF THE JOURNEY BACK (Harcourt Brace, 1973)
SASSAFRAS (Houghton Mifflin, 1983)

—Short Stories—
BITTER KNOWLEDGE (Scribners, 1964)
TALES OF THE OHIO LAND (Ohio Historical Society, 1978)
DUBIOUS PERSUASIONS (Johns Hopkins Univ. Press, 1981)
CRAZY WOMEN (Johns Hopkins Univ. Press, 1985)
GHOSTLY POPULATIONS (Johns Hopkins Univ. Press, 1986)

—Nonfiction—
COLLECTING RARE BOOKS FOR PLEASURE AND PROFIT (Putnam, 1977)
BOOKING IN THE HEARTLAND (John Hopkins Univ. Press, 1986)

—Poetry—
AN ALMANAC FOR TWILIGHT (Univ. of North Carolina Press, 1966)
IN A THEATER OF BUILDINGS (Ox Head Press, 1970)

JACK MATTHEWS

THE SMOKE OF INVISIBLE FIRES

I

Muttering, Paul Sullivan went to the front door and closed it against the cold October wind. His grandmother had left it open. She walked the house chanting, with tears glistening in her eyes. Martha, his grandmother, was inequitably old for only seventy-four. A dozen fuses had blown in her head. She was, he often thought, a foundering argosy of decay, varicosed and wrinkled. A woman who at odd moments held her hand up to her mouth in fear and sucked in her breath.

Paul walked into the kitchen, and Martha was sitting there mumbling. He was relieved to see that she was fully dressed.

"Have the Sisters come yet?" he asked. Conversation, he remembered reading once, is what the old and infirm crave.

His grandmother looked at him and belched. Her unblinking eyes seemed too large and curiously webbed with dust. Her hair was pushed back in a stringy gray bun, as if waiting to be clutched and yanked by some malicious boy.

Saturday afternoons were bad. Sundays were bad. Other days he could escape to work. Upstairs, in an unwrinkled bed, his mother lay like the pupa of a moth. Silent and astronomically alone, as he thought of her. Maybe he should comb her hair this morning.

"No, today the nuns don't come until after breakfast," Martha said—over-pronouncing the words because she was proud of possessing information.

"Have you been hiding money again?" he asked, narrowing his eyes.

"No, God love you!" she said, suddenly shimmering with her own brand of bargain mart piety. "And I haven't found that letter you're always asking me about, either."

"What letter?"

"Never mind, if you don't remember!"

Yesterday, he had come upon her purse lying open on the floor. Picking it up, he had seen a piece of bread wadded up in it. Against the fear of starvation, no doubt. Last week, mistaking one of his T shirts for a pillow case, she had tried to put it on a pillow.

Sometimes people said it was disturbing that his mother was often in the house alone with such a woman, even if she was her own mother. It was his grandmother, really more than his mother, who had kept him from returning to the university. But Father Powers had once interrupted his anecdote about Saint Columba to say he didn't have to quit; the Sisters could take up the slack, he said. But Father Powers might have believed all things are possible with Faith.

To have her hospitalized, it was understood, but never said, would be a betrayal. Also more expensive than they could afford.

Paul never argued the point. He accepted the situation with a sense of perverse vengeance. He had taken a job clerking in a sporting goods store, and had written scarcely coherent letters to his girl friend, Helen, telling her that he couldn't even consider marriage now, "until things changed."

"You don't have to hide your money," he said patiently, puffing on a cigarette and filling the percolator with scoops of coffee. His grandmother was standing half-hidden by the pantry door. It seemed he was always saying this to her. He struck a match along the rough cast-iron grating of the left burner and ignited the gas. It puffed into a perfect corolla of flame beneath his hand, and he turned to her.

"You'll never have to take a long trip, either. So for God's sweet sake, stop bellyaching!"

She was his mother's mother, he had to remind himself; and for the most part she had gotten childish after the accident . . . and now wandered about the house awash in a sloppy, self-pitying mire of anxiety. She was certain that someone was going to take her away from her poor helpless child, her daughter, who had not seen the light of day, or heard the sound of a human voice, for over eleven months. As for her grandson, she hardly remembered him.

Drinking his coffee, he turned on the radio. There might be some cheerful music for the old woman. She bit her lip and wound a loose strand of gray hair around her index finger.

Then he walked upstairs to his mother's room, calling out, "Tell me when the Sisters come."

His mother lay in the darkness, breathing silently. Paul sat upon the edge of the bed, picked up a hair brush, and commenced stroking the hair, as he'd been instructed. The Convent was only a block away (such convenience was uncanny—almost like an act of God, they all said), and the Sisters saw that the sick woman was cleaned daily and taken care of. Once every two weeks they washed and set her hair. They put a rubber mat under her head and wrapped a bath towel, rolled like an innertube around her neck.

Now she lay easy in her prison of sleep. At first, small frowns and twitches had surfaced on her face, like wind ruffles on a lake. Gradually, as if from obscure acquiescence, they had ceased. They had been replaced, the Sisters sometimes told themselves, by a look of radiant serenity.

And then this was replaced by a neuter look, as of a corpse before the mortician arranges the features pleasantly. Her fingernails and hair continued to grow. In the mornings, there were colorless deposits on the insides of her closed eyes. But nothing about her moved. Her brain, the doctor had told him, was practically dead. The accident had broken her back and damaged the conscious part of the brain, but a tireless impulse in the motor regions still sent out its message to the heart and lungs to stay alive.

Paul opened the blinds and gazed at her face. Her hair was spread fan-like on the pillow. Her jaw hung slack. One eyebrow seemed slightly higher than the other. The eyebrow was the only deviation from perfect symmetry. The face was as perfect and empty as a shell washed onto a lonely beach.

"Paul! Paul!"

It was his grandmother calling from downstairs. He heard the stairs creak with the weight of two people climbing them, and he knew it was the Sisters.

As usual, Sister Veronica went into the bathroom to wash her hands, and Sister Clementine came straight into the bedroom, lifting her fat little chin high in the air.

"Hello, hello," she said rapidly; and as always gazed at some spot above his eyes, as if speaking to his hair. Then she turned and looked at his mother.

Paul watched for an intimation that Sister Clementine had seen a change in her color. Perhaps, for the barest instant, a shadow flicked across the glassy merriness in her eyes, but it was gone so fast that Paul wasn't certain it had really been there at all.

He looked again at his mother's face. And now that Sister Clementine was here, he was sure that his mother's complexion had gotten grayer.

He went to the small upholstered maple chair and sat down. At this moment, Sister Veronica came in.

Her tiny nose was red and freckled, and it tilted up saucily. There was nothing else in her face to indicate buoyancy. She tended to be ill-natured, and she was unnecessarily short with old Martha's whining.

"Don't you *ever* leave any doors open around that helpless woman lying there!" she had angrily commanded his grandmother one day. Martha had argued incoherently, even after Sister Veronica had hurried out of the room, dragging a contrite Sister Clementine with her.

Apparently, Sister Veronica pictured herself as a kind of harsh-tongued angel who tries to protect people by scolding and bullying them. Only she wasn't intelligent enough to distinguish among her subjects, and such a treatment with Martha was like running an electric mixer through the old woman's hair.

Now, Sister Veronica cast black looks at Paul, while she fussed about the bed.

"I suppose it's time for me to leave," he said, standing up.

They said nothing, so he walked out of the room, feeling that they considered him as useless as he considered himself, and secretly despised him. Rather, Sister Veronica must feel this way. Sister Clementine seemed incapable of objecting to anyone.

Would it have been easier if *he* had been like Sister Clementine?

II

"Pray," Father Powers had said. "Not for her to get well, but for the strength to bear up under whatever is given to you."

"God's blessing on all of you," the Sisters said.

The bell tolled in the cathedral tower two blocks away; time passed; Martha—his senile and demented grandmother—paced the house hiding nickels, quarters, and dimes in vases, ash trays, books, and even under the carpet.

"If I had been God, I would never in a million years have let something like this happen," Paul had told Father Powers one day. "Not even if she had been a whore or drunkard. Do you realize how everyone loved her?" Even as he said this, he realized that his expression of devotion to his mother was at the moment vitiated by his chronic, if unfocused, resentment of the priest.

"What particular aspect of Adam's navel are we talking about now?" Father Powers had said, drawing a cigarette out of the center of his mouth and tilting his head to the side. The old man sat there in his study with one leg thrown over the arm of a large vinyl-plastic chair. "Have I missed a turn? Did I feel a lurch as the subject changed?"

Paul did not answer.

"Just how *would* you run the world if you were in charge?" Father Powers asked, with the famous little V-shaped Irish grin on his face. He had probably meant that sarcasm as a kindness, too, to jar Paul out of his trance of self pity. Father Powers was a chain-smoker, and Paul was convinced that this was partly because the old priest knew that cigarettes really do cause lung cancer. Not suicide, *as such;* rather some more oblique insult to the Holy Spirit.

"I don't know about the world," Paul had said, his hands trembling on the arms of his chair. "I can only speak about this."

"So there you are. Only *that,* which takes in all we can know of theology." He snapped his fingers. "Naturally, you're positive."

"It was the specific way it happened, too. I can't ever forget that."

"Ah," Father Powers said, his face turning sad. The volume of his voice went down still lower, so that he was almost whispering as he looked over Paul's shoulder—as if at someone else—and said gently: "I was wondering when you would bring that up. I could feel it coming. It fell like a shadow over my thought just then. Of *course* you can't forget it, son. God knows. God knows. How *could* you?"

"I just don't want to talk about it. You know all about it—everybody does. I get the feeling that total strangers could tell by just looking at me. I've gone over it too often. I've talked it to death. Don't think I don't know that. I don't see any further need to bring it out in talk."

Father Powers sighed and slapped his knee hard with his open hand. "That's where you're wrong. You *haven't* talked it to death. It needs bringing out before it poisons you like decaying food inside your body."

"Food?"

"Never mind that. Like this infernal cigarette I'm smoking, God help me. A ten-penny coffin nail if I've ever seen one! It accumulates; the tar does. You're not guilty at *all*, in any recognizable theological sense. Even Cicero knew better—a Dago and a pagan. Don't you think he could divide act and intention? No one could ever for a moment doubt that you loved your mother."

"I could have had it fixed," Paul said miserably, trapped somehow into repeating this drab litany to a man he was half-convinced (or convinced half the time) was nothing more than a glib and flamboyant charlatan . . . or perhaps a fool nailed to a dead Faith.

"The door?"

He nodded.

"Hindsight is always there to torment us," the priest said with a sigh. "The Hound of Hindsight!" When he was giving comfort, Father Power's large jaw seemed to grow heavy and loose, and his drowsy look of pity hinted at the possibility that he was being gradually drugged by his own rhetorical extravagances.

"How many things could we improve upon," he continued, taking sudden refuge in the theoretical, "if we could only do them over again. But the sins that are really . . . really *stubborn* are those we just can't bring ourselves not only to extirpate, but regret. Or even acknowledge. The sins we still secretly, insidiously *love*."

"I regret it all right."

"I know you do, Paul. I was just thinking out loud. Generalizing."

"And I *swear* I told her about that door a thousand times! That it was sprung and couldn't be trusted. Not to *lean* against it!"

"I'm sure you did. Of course. No doubt at all."

"But I suppose I *did* swerve too fast."

"What's too fast, Paul? If the door hadn't sprung open suddenly, causing your mother to fall out onto the street, smashing the back of her head on the pavement, would you have brooded about turning the corner too fast? And what if you'd hit that car that pulled out in front? Answer me. Would you?"

"How could I ever know that?"

"Hitting that other car might have killed the both of you!"

"Sure."

"A truly bizarre and tragic accident," Father Powers whispered, shaking his head. "But there are simple rules, Paul; and the rules say you're innocent. A moron could understand them. Take comfort in them; the strongest wisdom lies in the most obvious facts. You've never seemed to understand that."

"I'll never be able to forget."

"Now you sound like a popular song," the old priest replied, jumping to his feet and rubbing his hands together vigorously. "Why don't we take up our old chess games again? I used to look forward to our Thursday nights. I believe I could take you four out of five, the state you've gotten yourself into now. We'll pick up the chess games and have my old bat of a housekeeper bring us a couple of bottles of beer. Maybe tell dirty stories."

Father Powers laughed explosively and licked his lips. His gray crewcut glistened like tiny silver feathers in the dim light of the study, and his face was covered with slabs of hard pale meat. He had known Paul's mother all his life, and had often referred to her as a real darling.

He was something of a cynic for a priest. But an Irish cynic. The women of the parish whispered about his manners, and the things he said, but found him thoroughly attractive. Underneath everything, however, people sensed that he was something of a tormented man. He had occasional, surprising dark moods that he didn't bother to hide, giving him a sudden, incomprehensible dignity.

"I wouldn't give a nosedropper full of booze for a priest that wasn't troubled by his own humanity," he would tell people at other times, when he was "himself."

Paul's contempt for the old priest was a misery to him. Father Powers' Irishness was appalling—a full-time occupation that left very little for his parish or priesthood. His love for rhetoric, melodrama, and resonant cliche* was surely his true faith . . . and yet, behind the stentorian formulae and specious profundities, there was an occasional glimpse of another Father Powers—canny and ageless, and wiser than any conceivable serpent.

"Mother love," he said now, drawing on his cigarette and winking one eye as he contemplated both the subject and the difficult young man before him, "is a wonderful and mysterious thing. It shares in the great and puissant yearning, no less, that we feel for the love of the Holy Mother."

"I know," Paul said, frowning and turning his head away.

"We're all scheduled to die. Death is the big thing; even—properly considered—the *great* thing . . . what difference does it make, *sub specie aeternitatis*, how it comes?"

"If she were really dead, it would be better in some ways. I wouldn't have to look at her."

But the thought flushed him with a deep and hideous feeling of guilt, as tangible as an odor, and he felt sick with fear.

In his mind, he fervently took back what he'd just said.

III

"All's not well," his grandmother was saying. "God love you, there's trouble!"

Paul was in the basement, putting clothes in the washer. Martha stood at the top of the steps, the light behind her silhouetting her figure. Her wild hair glowed like a thorn bush after the flame has suddenly died down. Her face was so dark that Paul could not see her features at all.

"It'll be all right," Paul said, without even bothering to ask what was bothering her.

"Not well, not well, Paul," she said. At least she knew his name in her present state.

"What isn't well, then?" he asked angrily, slamming a dirty shirt into the washer door.

"*Things!*" she cried. "They're going to take me away, but you won't believe me. It will be a long, long trip, but little you care! A distant place, mysterious. Then they steal my money. And don't ever irritate the Sisters. Where would we be without them? *Pray* for them, *I* say!"

"All right," Paul said. "I'm tired of hearing about it."

"Not only that," she said, "the Sisters haven't come yet."

"Is it time?" Paul asked.

"Of *course* it's time. Past time. They're supposed to be here early to give her a bath."

Paul stared at her a moment, deciding that her mind had scrambled up out of the sea of madness she foundered in, onto an unexpected little island of sense.

"What time is it?"

"It's after four!" she cried. "Why, they're an hour late! A whole hour!"

Paul went over to his watch he'd taken off and laid on an old table, and saw that she was right. It was four-fifteen.

"They'll come," he said. "You can depend on them."

"It isn't them," Martha said hollowly. "It's not them."

Paul turned the washer on and went up the steps toward his grandmother. She backed up cautiously as if she were afraid he might shove her backwards or strike her in the face. In the light of the kitchen, her lipstick was a thin, erratic smear on the inside of the mouth, leaving most of her lips unpainted. Her eyes squinted in pain, as if she were staring suspiciously into a reality so glaring that it seared her vision.

"No, it's not the Sisters, God love them! It's *him*. The priest!"

"Father Powers?" Paul said.

"Yes, *him*. Whatever his name is. The priest!"

"Everybody likes him," Paul said, starting into the other room.

But the dam in her thoughts broke, and she stood wailing in the kitchen. "There's something about that man I don't trust!" she cried. "He's keeping the Sisters away from us. *That's* what he's doing!"

"Stop that!" Paul yelled from the front room.

"Well, what's he doing then, if he isn't doing that?"

Paul thought a moment, then shouted: "Writing his famous biography of Saint Columba!"

"Go on! Hide my money, you and that priest. See if I care. Do you know I find nickels and dimes and quarters all over the house? Under the pillows on the sofa, in the ashtrays, under the rug, in the closet, in the pockets of old coats? *Do you know that?*"

"It's *you* who hide them there, you damned loony!" Paul yelled. "Now shut up, will you!"

The door bell rang. Paul went to it and admitted Sister Veronica and Sister Clementine.

"I'm sorry we're late," Sister Clementine said. "We were held up because of some problems with our furnace. It's broken down again, and . . ."

"So you escaped from him, did you?" Martha said. She was standing in the entrance to the kitchen; and although she had spoken no louder than normal, her voice sawed sharply across Sister Clementine's explanation.

"Him?" Sister Veronica asked. "Who's this we're talking about *now?*"

"She thinks Father Powers kept you there . . . just to keep you away from Mother."

"Oh," Sister Veronica said. "So that's what she thinks! So *that's* the score of the old ball game, is it!"

"Why can't you talk to *me?*" Martha said, wringing her hands and starting to cry. "Why did you have to say that to my grandson, when *I'm* the one who needs information? *Nobody* gives me information, you know! But they steal my money. Information is power, and so's money."

"Now, now," sister Clementine said, smiling shinily into the old woman's face.

"Let's get down to business," Sister Veronica said.

"I hate him," Martha shouted. "I don't trust him. There's something wrong with the man!"

"Father Powers is a fine priest," Sister Clementine said. But of course, she would have said that about any priest. She couldn't believe that there was any point in criticising another. Facts had nothing to do with it, in Sister Clementine's thinking. It was simply a question of kindness.

Sister Veronica didn't seem to think the subject was worth venturing an opinion on—not the priest himself, exactly, but this particular attack upon him from a mad woman.

"Hurry up," she said to Sister Clementine. "We've got work to do."

The two of them went upstairs.

IV

The chess games were impossible. Father Powers talked upon many topics, seeming to forget not only the game, but his audience as well. Eventually, Paul would find an excuse to leave the husky old priest sitting there over the chess board, holding his cigarette melodramatically between his thumb and finger, like a gangster in an old-time movie.

But they did play a crazy game of handball one day in the high school gym of St. Al's. Father Powers insisted upon it. Paul favored the old man shamelessly, afraid for his heart. Classes were in session; and once during their game, Paul heard the bell, and then the sound of hundreds of footsteps pounding in the halls as classes changed. As always, there were no voices or sounds of conversation to be heard.

He stopped, holding the ball, and turned to the priest. "You know," he said, "one thing I always resented here at St. Al's was the regimentation. I always felt that at least we should have been allowed to talk in the halls while we were changing classes. It isn't as if we were little kids. Or cadets in a military school."

Father Powers turned to Paul, still panting—his face glistening with moisture and his body exuding an odor of male perspiration. Jokingly, he had complained of being "out of two things: practice and breath."

"The students?" he asked.

"Yes."

The priest smiled grimly, and leaned over to pick up a towel. He commenced to wipe his hands and said, "Paul, you're a born revolutionary. A real constitutional sorehead and belly-acher. *I* can't make sense out of it. Essentially a good Catholic, mind you, underneath all the fire and hokum—but a born revolutionary. It's a paradox, but there you are. All I can say is, it's a good idea you changed your mind about becoming a priest."

"They still ought to be allowed to talk, it seems to me," Paul said, bouncing the ball on the floor and following it closely with his eyes.

"I do wish you'd gone to Notre Dame, though. I *do* wish that! Even if you had decided against becoming a priest . . . which—I repeat—was a good decision. You just don't have the vocation. Now if it were the perverse pursuit of *loneliness* we were talking about . . . or a certain bittersweet, narcissistic, hyper-emotional *masochism.* . . ."

"Why don't you come off it!" Paul said angrily, snatching the ball with a swift hook of his hand.

But Father Powers was not through, and he seemed contentedly oblivious to the effect of his sarcasm. "There's no reason you have to *incarcerate* yourself as you've done. Why do you think the Sisters come over there every day if not to lift your burden a little? Why, in God's name don't you go out and drink a beer or two, associate with people, have a girl friend, participate in the large life of church and community!"

"Come off it, will you?"

"And think of how many people there are to argue with out there in the great world! Think of the *arguments* you're missing."

"All right, all right!"

Father Powers shook his head, smiling tightly. "No, it's a blessing that you didn't go into the priesthood. Although we do need an occasional *Advocatus Diaboli!* . . ." he frowned momentarily at the figure, and then added, "as it were."

"I've forgotten all about that, long ago. Even about going to Notre Dame."

"People don't ever really *forget!*" the Priest whispered. Don't you know that?"

"I guess I did once, but I'd forgotten," Paul said.

Father Powers lifted his chin in a silent small-mouthed laugh. Then he whipped the towel around in the air. He was still breathing heavily, standing there flatfooted and tired.

"No, you don't have the vocation," he said. "The priesthood would have ruined you sooner or later, most likely. It can be a blessing or a curse, largely depending upon what you can bring to it. Some of us . . . some of us fail miserably in our commitments. And I'm not talking about my book on St. Columba, you may be sure! One can hardly measure the difficulty, the trouble. . . ."

Father Powers stopped talking. He stood there holding the thick towel in his hands as if it were a vestment he was about to put on. His hands were finally wiped dry, now; he often said he couldn't stand to have his hands wet or dirty.

"And there's another thing," he said, lowering his voice as if about to utter something shameful. "You're far too soft for it. You're a sentimentalist, Paul, which is something no priest can afford to be."

"I'd say it's the other way around, in your case; it seems to me you're *all* sentiment."

"I'm not talking about sentiment; I'm talking about *sentimentality*. Do you think I'll ever forget the story about the cat?"

"What story?"

Father Powers waggled his finger at him. "Don't pretend to an old actor! *You* remember."

Paul nodded. "The cat I ran over that day and killed."

"Squashed him flat as a pancake, you told me."

"That wasn't confession, don't forget."

"Of course I haven't forgotten. Only I wonder if it wasn't. I've seldom seen such moral shock . . . such contrition. You came and talked to me in my study—your face as white as a bishop's underwear! And what was it, after all? You'd hit a cat, driving that car of yours; and you acted like a man who's just discovered he's made a hole in the universe!"

"I remember."

"Of course you do. And I told you a cat has nothing in the way of a soul; all it has is life. Do you remember?"

"Of course I remember."

"And while God may mark the sparrow's fall, he surely can't be what you'd call *surprised* by it. Nor shocked, we may presume. He doesn't miss a day's work. He doesn't take time off for mourning. Because all things mortal . . ."

"Et cetera," Paul repeated, nodding. But at that instant, he noticed that the old priest's face had gone dark with sadness—as suddenly as white paper turning gray under water. As if his mind had accidentally touched something else. At moments like this, he looked much older than he normally did . . . the heavy wrinkles about his eyes giving him a secretive, oblique, almost defeated look.

"My father always wanted me to go there."

"What," Father Powers said.

"To Notre Dame," Paul said, bouncing the ball again, his eyes following it up and down, from the glassy gym floor to his hand—back and forth. "You just said you wished I'd gone to Notre Dame. And I said, my father always wanted me to go there."

"Yes," the priest said. "I know. Of course. Only . . . well, the main thing is that you go back to the university. I see things in you that are frightening, Paul. And I say it as your friend and priest. You show a trait that—it depresses me to say—is peculiarly Irish. The best way I can describe it is, it's a stylish allergy to success of any sort."

"I've heard that before, too."

"Not from me, you haven't."

"Not directed to me personally, but I've heard you hold forth on it. It's one of your favorite topics. An Irish topic, I might add; and one that you're very successful at."

Father Powers laughed thinly. "You're also evasive. What I want to say is, do you know you might live your whole life and never find out how smart you are?"

Paul snatched the ball with another swift hooking motion, and turned to face the old man. "You never did like my father, did you?"

The priest opened his eyes wide. "What a surprising thing to say! You *are* a young devil, aren't you! A real troublemaker in our midst!"

"Well, did you?"

"Whatever gave you such a fantastic idea?"

"Just casual remarks. Expressions. I've put them together."

"I once knew a man," Father Powers said, once more smiling and evidently feeling in control, "who bought a boat kit and made wooden porch furniture out of the materials."

"That doesn't answer my questions."

"You are as outspoken and wrong-headed as anyone I've ever seen!" Father Powers said. But there was a faint smile on his face as he said it.

"You still won't answer, will you?"

"About your father? Yes, I'll answer this way: he was a very troubled man. I think that's the first thing we have to understand about those things he did that brought so much unhappiness to so many people. Troubled. How much was moral and how much diseased—beyond his control—only God could judge. *I* certainly will not presume to judge. So we'd best not think too much about it. Only lament the loss of his good qualities, the suffering he brought to himself *and* others. . . ."

"He *did kill* himself, you know!" Paul said angrily. He tossed the ball away without looking. "That's a sin, I've been led to understand. He drank too much for at least ten years. Probably committed adultery. . . ."

Father Powers snorted. "*Probably?* Now you're judging a man you scarcely knew on *probability?*"

"I may not have known much about him," Paul said, "But I've reaped the harvest of his rich cultivation, don't think I haven't; and you can't say. . . ."

Father Powers gave an abrupt laugh, which ended in a sneer. "Now it's rhetoric, is it? Oh, aren't you the holy suffering one, though!"

Paul was silent for an instant. Then he turned and strode angrily from the gym, knowing—as did the priest who watched him leave—that nothing essential had changed between the two of them.

V

Death, which Father Powers had said comes to all, released Paul Sullivan and his mother from their mutual and unnatural bondage on a cold November night.

In the morning, Paul had gone upstairs to brush her hair. He sat on the edge of the bed before he noticed something different about the face beside him.

When Sister Veronica and Sister Clementine entered the house shortly afterwards, old Martha was weeping on the davenport, not because her daughter had finally died, but because she was afraid she would have to take a long trip soon, to a destination she could not understand.

When Paul told the Sisters, it was harsh Sister Veronica who had to wipe tears from her eyes, perhaps vindicating her innermost opinion of herself. Sister Clementine only smiled dimly and sadly, and said her beads.

Paul phoned Father Powers and waited.

The burly old man parked in the driveway and left his car door swinging open. He walked into the house and stopped for a second to stare at Paul without speaking. Martha was standing motionlessly there beside him, as expressionless as an unlit floor lamp.

Father Powers' clipped hair looked mussed, somehow, and his eyes were red from a nasty head cold he'd been complaining about. Still without speaking, he went upstairs, and then returned in a few minutes. Paul was sitting on the sofa with his elbows on his knees and his head down. Martha was still standing motionlessly beside him.

"Well?" Paul asked, looking up.

Father Powers lighted a mentholated cigarette and exhaled audibly. With the back of his hand he wiped his left eye, which was watering from his head cold.

Martha suddenly pitched forward and trotted slowly into the kitchen with her head down.

"I've known her all her life," Father Powers said. "We practically grew up together; although I was older, of course." Carefully, he exhaled smoke with his lips close together. Then he sat down in an upholstered chair across from Paul, and threw his leg over the arm.

"It's all over," Paul said.

"Well, I understand how you feel," Father Powers said. "She was a wonderful woman. She's better off now than she has been for a long, long time. But of course, you know that."

Father Powers nodded, laid his cigarette in the ashtray, pulled his leg off the chair arm, and put his elbows on his knees. Then he nuzzled his face in his hands. Paul could hear him take two deep breaths through his thick fingers. Suddenly, the priest dropped his hands and looked at him out of eyes that were merely red and tired-looking from the cold.

"She *was* beautiful, Paul! A mere glance at her was like stepping on a patch of ice! I remember, when she was about twenty-five that . . . God help me, but I almost left the priesthood for the mere *thoughts* of her!"

"I know," Paul said. "You've mentioned that before."

"Yes. Well, that's irrelevant now, anyway. Consider her. She is simply better off by *any* standard."

"I know," Paul said, and then surprisingly he smiled. "There is a kind of relief in it."

The Priest nodded. "Yes, yes, to be sure."

"I have one favor to ask of you," Paul said.

Father Powers lifted his cigarette, took a drag on it, and then stubbed it out. He raised his thick eyebrows. "And that is?" he asked.

"Find a home for *her!*" Paul jabbed his thumb toward the kitchen.

"She's your grandmother. Don't forget that."

"Listen, I'm not in any mood for moral instruction!"

Surprisingly, Father Powers did not get angry. He stared meditatively at the far wall, as if it were something that required compassion and deep understanding.

Then he looked back at Paul a second, closed his eyes, and said, "I'll do what I can about her. She really should be in a nursing home. But remember this: you'll have no family at all. Nobody to bother you. Nobody at all. You'll be alone. It's not all good not to be bothered."

"All right," Paul said. "I'll remember."

The priest opened his mouth as if about to say something else, but then he clamped his jaw shut and nodded. After which, he got up, and Paul escorted him out of the house.

On the porch, Father Powers turned around and said, "What about our old chess games?"

"I don't know," Paul said. "I can't seem to think about anything now. But, I'd appreciate if it you'd get to work on getting my grandmother into a sanitarium."

"I'll do what I can," Father Powers said, nodding. "Everything I can. Meanwhile, just one more thing . . ." He stopped and rubbed his hand along the brim of his hat, his inflamed eyes suddenly vague, as if he were about to go to sleep standing up.

"Yes?" Paul said. "What is it?"

The priest swallowed and turned to gaze out at the neighborhood. "The things you think are most tangible, most real . . . these things dissolve like sugar in water. And most of what we know of ourselves is among them. We're as vulnerable, and in most respects as worthless, as that cat you ran over in your car. So maybe the less tangible things have a chance. There's an odd but severe logic in this. Do you understand what I'm telling you? Because it's all we have."

"I guess so," Paul said. He felt that under the circumstances he would have agreed with just about anything the priest said.

Father Powers seemed satisfied, and he nodded. Then he went out to his car, and paused briefly at the open door, as if surprised to find he'd left it open.

After which, he got in, started the car, and backed it slowly out the drive. Without having once made any gesture to pray or otherwise offer Paul anything in the way of religious consolation.

VI

Father Powers kept his word, and within three weeks, Martha had been removed to a home conducted by the Sisters of Mercy, only forty miles away.

The event transpired almost mechanically, almost impersonally, for the old Priest and Paul did not see one another during this time, seeming to keep their distance from a tacit understanding that there was nothing between them waiting to be said or done.

Paul found himself working harder than ever in the sporting goods store, taking the details of his work more seriously than he could have believed possible only a month before. Often, in the evenings, he went to the library and read indiscriminately and passionately, as if somewhere there might be relevant information awaiting him.

When he telephoned Helen, and told her of all that had happened, he realized for the first time she had not even called or sent a card when his mother died. He interpreted this fact as a symptom of his basic indifference to her, in that he had not noticed it before, and did not greatly care now that it had finally occurred to him.

So he was batching it in his dead family's old house, gathering himself together, preparing to live again, to go out, to "become something."

One day, almost a month after his grandmother had finally taken that long-dreaded journey and entered the sanitarium, he was shopping in the local Kroger's store and came upon Sister Clementine. She seemed a little embarrassed to see him, and before he could even wonder at seeing her there alone, she said she had needed to purchase nose drops, and that was why she had come in. She appeared to regard the excursion as a great, daring, and possibly wicked adventure.

He thought briefly of teasing her, of saying that stuffy noses were often psychosomatic problems; but for some reason he did not. Partly, this was because of a distant look she got while they were still facing each other, with neither having given a sign of parting. Evidently, she was waiting to tell him something.

"How *have* you been?" he repeated.

Her eyes spiralled back to his, and she smiled vaguely. "Oh, we've been fine. Sister Veronica is still a saint in complainer's clothing. We are all getting along. Except for Father. But I suppose you've heard, haven't you?"

"No, I haven't," Paul said. "I haven't been going to Mass these days."

Sister Clementine smiled distantly and nodded. "Father Powers I'm speaking of."

"I know," Paul said.

"He's had a heart attack. He's in the hospital now. Recovering, thank God; but they didn't expect him to pull through for a while."

"God!" Paul whispered, looking down.

"The doctors didn't."

"What?"

Sister Clementine nodded encouragingly. "The doctors didn't expect him to recover. I was just explaining."

"Of course," Paul said.

"I'm sure he'd take it very . . . well, I'm sure he'd be pleased if you would come to see him. What I mean is, he has always thought a great deal of you. And your whole *family*, of course."

Paul nodded, biting his lip. Then he said, "Sure. I'll go. Where is he?"

"St Mary's," Sister Clementine said.

"Where else," Paul muttered.

"Where else, indeed," the nun said, blowing her nose on a kleenex.

VII

Room 319, Coronary Unit of St. Mary's hospital—imitation Gothic, vintage, 1920.

Paul entered the room at exactly nineteen minutes after three, making a great thing out of the coincidence of the time and room number . . . hardly looking at the sick man as he explored the implications of the numbers, while the priest lay there comfortably waiting for him to work this nervous nonsense out of his system.

"You have an interesting flair for the superstitious," Father Powers said. "And I like you for it. It shows a potential gift for Faith, although it's true that few manage to make the critical transition."

"Don't preach to me," Paul said, finally managing not only to look straight at the priest, but to stare at him hard. "I didn't come here for that."

Father Powers' complexion was silvery, his eyes dark. He looked as strong as stainless steel. But the fact was, he was feeling sentimental. "Do you know," he said, "that I have now lived almost twenty years beyond my father's age at his death?"

"What?" Paul asked, unprepared for such a speculation.

"I am sixty-four years old," Father Powers said, shaking his head. "My father was only forty-five when he died. He *worked* himself to death, you might say. He worried over us all, neglected his health, his diet. . . ."

"Probably smoked too much," Paul said.

"It was heart with him," Father Powers said, nodding. He gave the word an overly Irish inflection, almost making it rhyme with "court."

"I came to find out how you are," Paul said uncomfortably. He was in no mood for death-bed eloquence or senile reminiscence.

"How can a man be older than his own father ever was?" the priest went on, oblivious to Paul's impatience. "Ah, but I am! And they have called me 'father' for over thirty years now. Thirty years."

"They say that's a long time."

"What will we do with the fathers? I ask you!"

"What do they do with us?"

Father Powers focused his eyes on the young man standing beside the bed and said, "God, but you *are* a cantankerous young savage, aren't you! If God had waited for your approval, the world would still be in its planning stages."

"Sister Clementine said you were here, so I thought I would come up and see you."

"Oh, you did, did you! Well, she is made of pure butter."

"She is made of sugar and deadly cholesterol, and you know it."

Father Powers smiled grimly at him, and shook his head. "How *is* it to be alone, after all this time?" he said in his famous haunted voice.

"What?" Paul asked.

"You heard me very well, I think. And I am a sick man, and in no mood for your little rhetorical games, my boy."

Paul nodded and mumbled to himself: "So this is the way it's to be."

But Father Powers gave no sign of hearing, and he said, "For the sake of God and Mary and all the motorboats in hell, will you sit down in a chair and talk *sensibly* for a change?"

The whimsical violence of this outburst impressed him, and he sat down, as if to await instructions.

"Only six short months ago," Father Powers said, looking up at the ceiling, "you were afflicted by three people: your mother who is now dead—*requiescat in pace;* your grandmother, who is now with the Sisters of Mercy (convinced, incidentally—as you probably know—that she has indeed been shipped out, *railroaded,* and is thus fulfilled in her darkest premonition that she would be forced soon into taking a long journey) . . . and last, and undoubtedly least in almost every conceivable hierarchy of value, your old family friend and priest (not necessarily in that order, you understand), the decaying clot of dignified garbage you see lying here before you under clean white hospital sheets, your erstwhile confessor, Father Powers."

Paul recrossed his legs and said, "Now, what was the question again?"

Father Powers raised his chin toward the ceiling and laughed a soundless laugh.

"What's the matter? Do you have a pain?"

The priest's expression changed suddenly to a frown, and he said, "For God's sake, boy, what's the matter with you! Have you forgotten *laughter?*"

"I didn't hear any."

"Well, *listen!*"

Paul got to his feet, shoved his hands in his pocket, and turned to look out the window. "Oh, God, it's like nothing's changed, nothing's ever happened. Or ever will."

"Oh, a great deal has happened," Father Powers said.

"Well, do me a favor, okay? Don't tell me about it!"

"I promise to you that I will not. For one thing, I couldn't."

"Listen, I don't want to hear about that, either."

"Nor that. Nor that."

"And that, too. That's another one."

Father Powers sighed dramatically. "Oh, you're a difficult young man! It seems to me I've seen your likes before, somewhere. I wonder what God meant by such as you!"

"I wonder too. And I wonder if the wondering is worth anything."

"Do you realize the fulfillment?" Father Powers recited dramatically. "She thinks that her fears have been fulfilled! She has taken that very journey she has feared so long! How complete her life must be!"

"Who, Martha?"

"Why, who else?"

"She's a thousand years old, and crazy as hell."

"Hell's not crazy. It's as rational as a row of brick houses or the behavior of politicians."

"I don't think I'm up to hearing about that, either," Paul said. He was still standing at the window, staring out upon the parking lot below.

"You're not up to much," Father Powers said sadly. "And here I was all set to tell you all I know. Like, how the doctors have said if my heart hadn't given up on me, my lungs would have. They've scolded me about my smoking cigarettes until I could have puked all over their green smocks. Their green *cassocks*. They're the priests of this exiguous world we live in today."

"I've heard you give that sermon many times."

"What they don't understand," the priest went on meditatively, "is my blessedly mysterious semantic web. When the things of this world forsake you, as they must inevitably, eventually do (and need I specify that this includes the body?), then a creature is thrown back upon the Inscrutables, capital I. The smoke from the body's bonfire, the fogs in the heart's suspicions."

"Listen," Paul said slowly. "I don't want to hear you drain yourself. Save it for your believers. I didn't come here to listen to things like that!"

"Why, of *course* you did!"

"Don't tell my why I came here. I came here as a friend, that's all. And I want to know how you're doing. That's *it*. I've had enough ghosts in my life to last me . . . well, for eternity."

"I couldn't agree more," the old man said, nodding.

"Which means it's time for me to go," Paul said.

"Of course. I didn't really think you'd stay this long. Don't forget, I know you."

For an instant, Paul didn't speak, and then he muttered good-by and went to the door.

But before leaving, he paused, turned, and said, "Listen, there is this one thing. Don't die. That's all. I mean, goddamit, I don't want you to."

"What a strange request!" Father Powers said, straining his head to the side so that he could see the other's face.

"I know. It sounds dopey. But there it is."

"There's a lot you haven't told me yet, is that it?" the priest said, smiling crookedly.

"Something like that. Only, the truth is . . . well, you probably know as well as anybody; I mean, I'm listening, too."

"How astonishing," the old man said. "I would never have guessed." He grinned with one corner of his mouth.

"And there's something else you should know."

"Such as?"

"About that cat you're always reminding me of."

Father Powers opened his eyes wide and stared at the young man standing beside his bed. "This one you ran down in your car and came to tell me about, as if you'd practically crucified him?"

Paul nodded. "I had to swerve the car before he could dodge out of the way. I can still hear his bones crunch under the wheel."

"Cat-icide!" the old priest wheezed, laughing.

"I personally didn't find it all that funny," Paul said, speaking tensely out of a white face.

"Of course you didn't. And it wasn't. Gratuitous cruelty is nothing to laugh about. That was a stupid, senseless thing you did!"

"You mean, you *knew* it was intentional?"

The old man took a deep breath. "I figured it to be *somewhat* intentional, or you wouldn't have come to me about it. You might have taken it to confession—saying you felt bad, and all that—but to bring it to me in my study . . . that was something else, my boy. In my study, you were under no pressure to tell the whole truth. Don't try to weasel with a weasel, Paul! I learned a great deal from that event. About you, about me, about the priesthood."

"I don't follow you."

"No, I don't suppose you do," Father Powers said comfortably adjusting the covers about his chest as Paul edged toward the door.

"Well, I'll be seeing you," he said.

"Good-by, good-by."

After he'd gone, the old man lifted his chin and pointed at the ceiling one of the last of those famous Irish smiles he would ever smile.

PHILIP F. O'CONNOR

Philip O'Connor has been teaching and writing in Ohio for twenty years now at Bowling Green State University where he co-founded and has directed the creative writing program. A native of San Francisco and a graduate of San Francisco State College and the University of Iowa, O'Connor has adapted to and adopted Ohio roots: "I've become on Ohioan. I feel its character and moods. I love to hang around after a hockey game listening to Ohioans talk, especially the older people who really love this place." His Ohioan connection goes so far as to include a deepened sense of history and order and has affected the very way he is, "I have adopted some of the customs and values of Ohioans. I speak in the clipped way Ohioans speak. I have found a sense of order here that I did not have in San Francisco."

His best selling novel STEALING HOME set in small town Ohio used both baseball and the Ohio Midwest to portray life, leading Webster Schott to declare in the NEW YORK TIMES: "STEALING HOME is extraordinary: a novel that seriously examines difficult questions about human motive and need." His earlier short fiction has appeared widely and has won acclaim for his values and his narrative skill. Stanley Elkins found the stories in his OLD MORALS, SMALL CONTINENTS, DARKER TIMES, "Excellent, written throughout with a sort of honed dignity which does credit to the author's kindly passion and gentle intelligence."

Novelist Christopher Davis marks well the sense of location O'Connor brings through his fiction, "capturing the life of people, the presence of places and the beauty of talk—so much so that we do not realize at once that we are in the very scene of our origins." O'Connor's new novel DEFENDING CIVILIZATION will be published later this year.

Like the telescopic portrait of Bonita Gamble Rumbard in his OHIO WOMAN, our story "The Voice of the Bird" reveals an entire life in a day, a telling portrait of the way we are. Our author fulfills well George P. Elliott's praise, "O'Connor has the true Irish gift of telling a tale for all it's worth. . . . His stories are taut and painful too; that is to say, they ring true."

AWARDS

Iowa School of Letters Award for Short Fiction
Story selected for BEST AMERICAN FICTION
Fiction judge for the Pulitzer Prize and Flannery O'Connor Prize

BOOKS

—Novels—
STEALING HOME (Knopf, 1980)
DEFENDING CIVILIZATION (Weidenfeld Nicolson)

—Novella—
OHIO WOMAN (Bottom Dog Press, 1986)

—Short Stories—
OLD MORALS, SMALL CONTINENTS, DARKER TIMES (Univ. of Iowa Press, 1971)
A SEASON FOR UNNATURAL CAUSES (University of Illinois Press, 1975)

PHILIP F. O'CONNOR

THE VOICE OF THE BIRD

What is wrong with me? Sheila wonders as she raises her eyes against another wave of dizziness. She's had a hard time following Father Rock's monthly address to the parish Ladies' Guild ("What Can You as a Mother Do for Mother Church?") and decides that the dizziness and lack of concentration are related.

Recently she failed to remember a parish meeting, lost two or three shopping lists, several times went from one room to another to get something, then forgot what she'd gone to get. Dr. Ferris told her the problem was too little sugar in her blood. "You need a sweetener to pick you up in the afternoons." She bought half-a-dozen peppermint patties and put them in her purse but, in the week since she bought them, she's remembered to take one only once.

She's about to reach into her purse for a pattie when she recalls she's just had a chocolate eclair, part of luncheon menu. *Little good it did,* she thinks.

She becomes aware that Father's talk has ended only when she sees the broad hands of Theresa Carmody on her left rise and begin beating each other like a sea lion's flappers. In contrast, the hands of Maria Gannon on her right are a pair of dancing jackrabbits.

Finally she raises her own hands but can produce only a few listless claps.

Maria turns and says, "That man never fails to stir me up!"

Sheila nods, ashamed that in her there's been no stirring at all.

After bowing toward the tables on his right, then toward those on his left—"Thank you. . . . Please, ladies! Thank you, thank you."—the priest raises his arms—"That's wonderful!

Thank you."—keeps them up until the applause begins to wear itself out. Then, using his fingers to comb back a swath of satin gray hair that fell to his temples when he bowed, he says, "I guess it's time for us to put all that good energy into some good works."

Sheila hears a hum of approval.

"Let's start by taking out a pen or pencil and a sheet of paper." He sends his eyes from table to table as Guild members reach for their purses, continues speaking only after the popping, clicking, shuffling sounds have stopped. "I'd like you to write down the ways, several at least, you think parishioners can best contribute to the financial good health of Agnus Dei."

Sheila's dizziness has now turned to drowsiness. She feels like putting her head on the table and taking a brief nap. *Wouldn't that be embarrassing?* she thinks, reaching for the carafe of coffee.

"You may list new approaches, as well as those we've used in the past. Just be sure that you, personally, are willing to contribute to the activities you put down."

Sheila was in charge of the used clothing sales during the campaign to raise money for a new priest's house. There were also cake sales, raffles, auctions, bingo games and car washes. Special second collections were taken every Sunday. Sermons often became pleas for giving. The result is a huge white edifice that stands on the hill above the church and school, dwarfing all the homes around it. Touring the place with other members of the Guild, Sheila found it more spacious within than it seemed from without. The first floor contains a large kitchen, dining room, three bathrooms, servant's quarters and several offices; the second a library, a meeting room and five bedrooms, each with its own bathroom; and the third an exercise room, a sun deck and a solarium with an unbroken view of the ocean. Only three priests reside there: Father Rock; his assistant, Father Carmody, Theresa's nephew; and Father Melvin, a lawyer who works at the chancery office downtown. "Maybe he's expecting John Kennedy or John the Twenty-third to come and visit," Joe remarked sarcastically after she told him about her tour. She twisted her mouth disapprovingly, yet was puzzled by the house, its size and grandeur. Why hadn't Father built a more modest home and used the left-over money to help the poor families of the parish or add badly needed classrooms to the school?

Yesterday she began crying at the vegetable stand in Al's Corner Store. Standing there, trying to decide whether to get parsnips or turnips for supper, she felt tears circling down her face. *My God!* She wiped her eyes with the sleeve of her coat, then stayed at the stand for several minutes, afraid someone would notice. Joe said you could always tell when she'd been crying. ("You look like a Jap.") Finally she made her way to the counter, where she picked up a couple of small packs of *Kleenexes* and tossed them in her shopping basket. She worried that Judy, Al's wife, who was working the cash register, might notice her eyes and ask what was wrong. She decided to cut her off. "I guess I'm coming down with one of those summer colds," she said. Judy glanced across, smiled indifferently and went on adding up the groceries.

"All right, ladies," Father says. "Time's up."

A few, including Theresa, go on writing.

"Ladies!"

Theresa puts her pencil on the table, turns and says, "I was never a fast thinker."

"I think fast enough," says Maria, "but I always find out later that someone else had better ideas."

Sheila has nodded after each of her table-mate's comments.

The old woman across from Sheila, a guest, has said nothing, but for the past few minutes she's been staring at Sheila. The expression Sheila first read as anger now appears to be something else. She isn't sure what. It reminds her of the look on Francis' face the first time he saw a man with a beard. He was only two, and she'd taken him into the Happy Clown's Diner downtown. No matter which way the poor man turned, Francis went around and stood in front of him. Finally Sheila had to pull the boy away. The old woman is studying her the way Francis studied the bearded man. *What does she see?* Sheila wonders.

"All right," says Father. "It's time for us to get down to business."

This morning Joe rumbled through the house in search of his second best pair of work shoes. (His best pair were on his feet.) "Help me find them, can't you?" Under the circumstances she couldn't. She watched him hop from one room to another, at times falling to all fours to check under a table or chair. His demands soon turned to undecipherable grunts. In the living room he stopped and in frustration banged both hands against the wall several times. He reminded her of Luke, the bigger of two gorillas down at Fleischacker Zoo. He never did find his shoes which meant that sooner or later he'd be returning for them. What matter? She felt only relief when he slammed the front door behind him!

She'd go the the beach. (How long has it been?) She'd take one of her paperback mysteries, stay until the cool afternoon breezes chases her home. She'd treat herself to an oversized hot dog and a bowl of chili at one of those "greasy spoon" places on La Playa. She put on a pair of cotton slacks and her loose-fitting rose-colored blouse. She dug out one of Francis' old windbreakers. She'd find a remote dune surrounded by rushes. If the sun managed to find its way through the fog, she'd pull back her blouse and let it put some color on her shoulders. How soothing the ocean is!, she thought, wondering what people who lived inland did to escape. Go to a river or creek, I suppose. She picked up her mystery, The Sunset Beach Murders, and was about to leave when the phone rang.

"Sheila, I want to be sure you're coming to the luncheon today," said Lydia Mellon, Guild President. "You're going to have to head a fund-raising committee. I don't yet know which one." Lydia always spoke rapidly, nervously, as if her car were running in the driveway. "We'll have to wait and see which ones he wants to form." Sheila had completely forgotten about the luncheon meeting. She didn't want to go, didn't want to have to answer questions about Joe's new bar or Francis finally being able to go the college. Above all, she didn't want to hear another speech by Father Rock. "Listen," she said. "Something's come up," "What!" snapped Lydia. "You know everything has to come together at today's meeting!" Sheila did know and was sorry. "A friend," she said. "She's gotten suddenly sick and wants me to be with her." The lie fell in her stomach like a cold stone. She tried to soften it. "Not terribly sick, but sick enough to need me." Was it anyone Lydia knew? "Oh, no. She lives across town." "Well," said Lydia, "if there's no great crisis, she can surely wait until after the meeting. We ought to be done by two. Listen, I'll even drive you there myself." Sheila assured her that wouldn't be necessary. "Good! We may even be done before two. Listen. You know how some of those others botch things up. I need you. Promise me you'll be there." Sheila closed her eyes. The sun wouldn't break through until early afternoon. There'd be plenty of time to enjoy it then. "I suppose . . . for that long, I can . . ." "You're a darling, Sheila! A real chum!" She heard Lydia *shuffling papers, no doubt looking up the next number she was going to dial.*

At eleven-forty, wearing her beige cotton coat, her Navy blue suit (too tight for her now), her white blouse with ruffled collar and her old but comfortable walking heels, she made her way up the hill toward the church, passing row after row of white and pastel-colored stucco houses, some identical to her own. She arrived at the gym just in time to help Lydia and a couple of other Guild officers open folding chairs and place them around the tables. "What would I do without you?" Lydia said.

After several women read their answers aloud, the priest says, "Well, that's just fine. Now let's put your ideas and mine together." He mentions a raffle ("Bill O'Brien, our resident *Buick* dealer, told me he's willing to let us have a Roadmaster at cost."), a spring festival ("Let's do it right, with crafts and games and such that will attract people from other parishes, and our non-Catholic friends as well. Maybe we can tie it in with the raffle."), a pizza sale ("Rocky and Ann Columbo were the most loyal of loyal parishioners before they moved to San Mateo. I have no doubt they're still with us in spirit. I'll ask them to provide the dough, sauce, cheese and pepperonis. If they agree, all you'll have to do is put the ingredients together. And, of course, sell the pizzas.")

Sheila turns her attention back to the guest.

Spindly, her movements abrupt, she came in late and took the only empty chair at the table. To the polite greetings of the other three, she responded with a quick and, it seemed to Sheila, unfriendly nod. She ate all of her salad but ignored the rest: the baked chicken, canned vegetables, mashed potatoes and chocolate cake. *Must be a million wrinkles in her face. How old? Eighty-five? Could be ninety.*

Sheila reaches across, picks up and extends the carafe. "Would you care for some coffee?"

The woman's puce-brown eyes leap away, then back. "That stuff's poison," she snaps.

"I'm sorry," Sheila says.

The old woman shakes off the remark. "All of it's bad," she goes on, "all that comes in packages, cans or bottles, all that doesn't come straight out of God's earth."

The other two at the table have turned troubled eyes on the stranger.

"People ask what's my secret. 'Eat nothing that comes out of a container,' I say. That's what it is."

"I have a feeling you're right," says Sheila.

"I *am* right." She sends a needle-like finger toward Sheila. "I had my son take me out of the home because of what they served. It wasn't real food at all. It made me tired and knotted up my bowels." She snaps her head to one side. "He didn't *want* me to come out. Said, 'The food is the same there as you'd get anywhere.' But it's not!"

Theresa's chair squeaks.

Maria turns to Sheila and blinks accusingly.

Sheila regrets having set the old woman off but is also curious. She leans forward as far as the bulk of her stomach will allow, and whisper, "Which home?"

"Oh, that Spanish looking place up there on El Rey Boulevard. I don't remember the name anymore."

"Mercy House," says Sheila.

"That's the one. They were dying like flies. I made a fuss and he *had* to take me out."

Joe and his brother delivered their mother, Katherine, there about a year ago. Its rooms were small and sparsely furnished and reminded Sheila of cells in a monastery. "It's not so bad," Katherine said the first time Sheila visited. "When the fog lifts, I can see a bit of the ocean." Sheila found the furniture, imitation Spanish Colonial, hard and uncomfortable. The windows were tiny and the lighting poor. She visited Katherine frequently, often bringing a loaf of sour-milk Irish bread, the kind Katherine herself had taught her to bake. Returning from an early visit, she suggested to Joe that his mother might prefer to live in their spare bedroom. She hadn't mentioned the possibility to Katherine, hadn't wanted to raise her hopes without being sure. He wasn't enthusiastic but said he'd bring the matter up the next time he visited. He visited rarely. A month passed. He never again got the chance. An attendant found Katherine dead in her chair by the window late one afternoon. It was a day, Sheila noted, when the fog hadn't lifted. Dr. Morrison, the Mercy house physician, assured Joe and his brother that their mother had experienced not a moment's pain. "Well, that's something to be thankful for anyway," Joe said.

The old woman studies Sheila through her hands, upraised like a church's cupola. "I won't go back," she says firmly. "I won't let him send me back."

"You shouldn't," says Sheila.

The woman's eyes now remind Sheila of the eyes of a beach sparrow that recently landed on the stunted cypress outside her basement window. After fluttering a bit, the bird peered in, right at Sheila. She eased toward the window, which was open several inches. The sparrow's tiny penetrating eyes followed as she slowly extended her hand under the window. She'd nearly touched the bird when, with eyes suddenly throbbing, it darted upward and vanished.

"I believe he's got another place in mind, just as bad. Worse, if it's the one I think it is. I've been there and seen the food."

Father has finished addressing the group. Sheila didn't notice him leaving the lectern but now sees his black suit descend like a curtain behind the old woman.

"Well, ladies . . ." He casts a smile from one to the other, showing large well-attended teeth. ". . . I guess it's time for you to get down to committee work." The smile widens.

"We're surely prepared for that now, Father," says Maria. "Thanks to you."

The priest nods, reaches down and touches the old woman's shoulders. "Come, Mother, It's time for your nap."

Sheila straightens, feeling as she does when at the end of one of her mysteries, she finds out what really happened.

The old woman shakes her head. "I'm having a nice conversation . . ." She points at Sheila. ". . . with that one."

The priest's dark eyes flash across.

Sheila shrugs, apologizing. She wishes to undo the conflict she's caused. Clearly the woman wants to stay. Quickly she suggests a compromise. "I'll take her up to the house later, Father, when . . . she's ready to go."

He shakes his head. "I'm afraid she has to leave now. You see, her doctor has ordered her to take a nap after lunch every day."

"*Your* doctor," the mother corrects.

"Yes. Well, he's a doctor nevertheless." He blinks rapidly.

In a moment the old woman rises out of her chair and stands limply beside her son. The priest isn't a tall man, perhaps five-ten, but beside her appears mountainous. Sheila notices superficial similarities: the arched eyebrows, sharp-tipped chins, a certain forward-tilt in the postures.

"Come now," he says.

The woman gives Sheila a pleading look, hesitates, then turns and takes her son's guiding hand. He leads her toward an exit.

"Wasn't it thoughtful of him to bring her to the luncheon?" says Theresa.

"At our table too," adds Maria. She laughs. "We didn't even know it!"

Sheila springs to her feet.

The other two at the table turn, startled.

"I'm just going to the bathroom," she says.

She heard a voice at the front of the house, got out of bed and made her way in darkness to the living room. Maybe Mrs. Ravetto next door was trying to get her cat out of their wistiria vines. She pulled the curtain from the big window but saw no one. She heard the voice again. She thought of going to the front door, opening it and saying, "Who's down there?" but there had been some burglaries in the neighborhood recently and she hesitated, afraid she might be shot if she startled an intruder. She thought of waking up Joe, but more than once she'd done that, then felt stupid afterwards. ("Can't you tell the sound of a voice from the sound of the wind?") She pulled back the curtain again and saw Francis standing just below her. The night was chilly, yet he wore no shirt, and, as he moved from beneath the window toward the curb, he seemed to be tottering. Where was his car? She rushed to the front door, opened it, called out, "Francis? What are you doing down there?" He stopped his singsong chant. "Francis?" she said softly. His only reply was a groan. She couldn't see him because of the walls on both sides of the stairway. She hurried down the steps and stopped. "Francis?" he turned. His eyes searched the space between them, finally reached her. He gazed as though she were a stranger. "Francis?" he repeated, as if he were calling himself. Then he took a step toward her and fell.

Only later, months later, did she, after working like a detective—questioning one of his friends, the doctor, finally Francis himself—piece together what had happened.

He and Martin and Martin's cousin, Jerry, had gone to a dance sponsored by the parents of the boys from St. Ignatius High for the girls from several Catholic girl's schools. Martin told her, "Francis started imitating different people, like one of our teachers and the cop who once gave him a ticket for going though a stop sign, a lot of people. He was very funny. We all laughed and kept him going." Martin and Jerry had arranged to leave with three girls they knew, but Francis wouldn't stop doing his voices, and one of the girls became frightened. "Why can't he be himself," she asked Martin. Martin didn't know. "He'll snap out of it," he said. But Francis didn't, and the girl refused to join them. "I think he's drunk or on dope," she said. "He wasn't either," Martin assured Sheila. She had no reason not to believe him. The other two girls wouldn't go if she wouldn't, and the three boys ended up by themselves. "That's when I knew something was really wrong." Martin admitted. "He said he was sick and stopped at the park. He kept using all those different voices, and, after a while he took all his clothes off except his shorts and went over to this drainhole near where we'd parked and knelt down and acted like he was trying to climb in. Jerry and I were afraid the police would come. We tried to get him to put his clothes back on, but I don't think he even heard us. Then he started talking to the hole. 'You won't like this, Mrs. McCarthy, but he kept saying, 'Mother? Mother? Mother?' " Frightened now, Martin and Jerry picked up Francis' clothes and led him to his car. Jerry took the wheel. "In the car he started making sounds like a baby. We took him straight home. We figured he'd be all right in the morning. Jerry would bring the car back then. We helped him out of the car, and he started up your stairs like he was going to make it in okay. I guess he didn't."

After helping him to his feet, Sheila guided him up the stairs. He didn't seem to recognize her. He chanted and made grunting sounds. These awakened Joe, who shuffled to the living room, where Sheila had left him on the sofa while she went to the kitchen to call Dr. Ferris. Searching for the doctor's number, she heard Joe talking: "Hey, answer me! What kind of booze did you guys have?" As she was starting to dial, Joe came into the kitchen. "That kid's dead drunk," he said. "He doesn't even have a shirt on." Sheila ignored him and dialed.

At the hospital Joe paced about the waiting room, asking questions she couldn't answer, questions she herself had: "Why is he acting like he doesn't know us?" "How come he's singing baby songs?" "What's wrong with him?" He sounded as frightened as she felt. Sitting there straight and rigid, she remembered how silent Francis has been lately, like a deaf person not aware of what was being said around him. And he didn't change even when Joe was having one of his tantrums. He'd been spending hours-at-a-time in his downstairs bedroom, she supposed to keep away from the arguments she and Joe had been having about whether or not he should quit his job at the brewery and put a down payment on a neighborhood bar. She'd thought Francis was merely protecting himself.

Finally the psychiatrist came into the waiting room and said Francis has had a mild nervous breakdown. He told them the prognosis was good, as good as one could expect when dealing with an illness like this. "He's young and in fine condition physically, but I'm afraid we'll have to keep him here for a while." Only after the doctor explained what he meant by "a while." ("six or seven months at least") did Sheila collapse in tears. She remembers Joe's hands, tender on her shoulders, remembers him saying, "He'll be okay. Don't worry. He'll be okay." How long had it been since he'd touched her go gently?

She lays her purse on the eye-level ledge in the girl's bathroom, quickly removes a *Kleenex* and dabs at her right eye, catching the first tear in time to keep it from finding its way onto her cheek. About to dab at another, she notices a dark fluttering movement, thinks it's a sign that her dizziness is about to return, then sees the movement again and realizes it's come from the narrow space between the ledge and the little push-out window that sits almost eye-level with the surface of the schoolyard. She leans forward, looks out, notices a cassock swishing in the breeze, sees Father Rock moving across the empty yard toward the steps that lead to the back door of the priest's house. She leans out further, sees the old woman several yards behind, erect, moving like a slow marcher.

The priest stops beside the first step, turns and looks back. He's frowning the way he does from the pulpit when an infant begins to cry or someone sneezes. He presses his open hand against the small of his back.

A steep sandy cliff separates the schoolyard from the house. Passage is by way of a zigzag set of stairs, about fifty in all. Sheila has climbed the steps several times, taking the gymnasium key to the housekeeper after a Ladies' Guild meeting. Each time she's imagined herself climbing the steps of one of those great Rhine River castles she saw on postcards years ago, the ones Joe sent her when he was a sergeant in the Army stationed near Munich. After his discharge he spoke about his happy days in Germany and said that someday he'd take her there. She said she wanted to explore one of those castles. This trip never came about.

The mother, still in her slow march, reaches her son, brushes past him, grips the wooden hand rail, raises one foot, then the other, onto the first step. The priest waits until she's gone up several steps, then, shaking his head, grasps the rail, turns and starts up behind her. He moves with stops and starts. When they reach the small back porch, he turns, glances at the schoolyard, turns back, reaches into his pocket, removes a set of keys, leans over his mother and inserts one of the keys in the door.

She tilts her head to one side and says something.

He forcefully pushes the door open.

She doesn't step forward.

He grabs her shoulders and pushes her hard over the threshold.

She fades, staggering, into the darkness beyond.

"My God!"

He turns, scanning the empty schoolyard, turns back and steps into the house.

Sheila backs away from the window, swings about, first toward the small sink near the door, then to the door itself. She wishes she'd stepped away moments sooner. She feels paralyzed.

"Sheila?"

It's a voice from the other side of the door, the voice of a woman, a voice she doesn't recognize.

"Hurry, dear! Lydia is forming the committees."

I must get back, she thinks but doesn't move.

"Sheila?"

She can't make herself go.

With money from the family savings account plus Katherine's small legacy, Joe, whose persistence had worn down Sheila, made a down payment on a neighborhood bar and quit his job at the Lucky brewery. He kept the old name, Sea and Surf, opened for business a few weeks after Francis' breakdown.

Though both the previous owner and the real estate man had persuaded him he could use the loft above the bar for extra income, he was able to rent it only twice during the first two months, once to a neighborhood social club and once to someone who wanted an inexpensive wedding reception. He frequently complained to Sheila about the room, stopped complaining only after a woman he called "The Gypsy" walked in.

"It was near closing time," he told Sheila the next day. "She was already drunk and could hardly give her order. I knew what she really needed was coffee, and that's what I brought her." He said she looked younger than her age, which turned out to be twenty-six. "Too damned pretty to be staggering around in the streets at that hour, for sure." He'd walked to the back to finish his dice game with the regulars but soon noticed her head on the bar beside the coffee cup. He returned to the front, shook her until she woke up and made her drink the coffee, having to hold the cup to her lips. He'd broken up the dice game, and the regulars started leaving, one by one.

"Where do you live," he asked, thinking he'd drive her there after closing.

"Got no place," she told him.

"Everyone's got some kind of place."

"Not me."

She told him her story. She'd come from Nashville with a man, not her husband, a singer who hadn't made it in the music business. He figured San Francisco would change his luck and invited her to join him. She wanted to get away. Her husband of six years, a day cook, beat her and their children frequently. "Least once a week," she said. She pulled back her blouse and showed Joe some scars around her shoulders. "They ain't the worst ones neither." To get out of the house when her husband was around, she'd taken a waitress job in a small club, which is where she met the singer. "It got to be a dream, getting out of there," she said. So big a dream she left her two kids, one age nine and one age four, with her mother. "He don't like kids," she said, meaning the singer. "Tonight I told him I wanted to get a job and send for them. That's when he kicked me out."

Joe couldn't take her home because she had no home. And he couldn't send her out on the streets. "There was that loft upstairs and here was her," he said. He poured her another cup of coffee and took the half-sofa from the back corner of the bar all the way up the stairs. He got an old picnic blanket out of the truck of the Pontiac, made a pillow out of a couple of towels and told her she could stay the night. He wasn't stupid. He cleaned every cent out of the cash register before going home. He took a chance that she wouldn't drink the liquor.

After waking up around noon the next day and telling Sheila about "The Gypsy," he said, "Now listen to this plan I have and tell me that you think."

Until then, he explained, customers who sat at one of the four round tables or on the half-sofa had to come up to the bar to order their drinks. When he was busy at the bar, people sometimes became impatient and walked out. "Suppose I make her a waitress. She can live upstairs free, use the sink and toilet up there and keep what she makes on tips."

Sheila answered with hesitation: "I think you'd be asking for trouble."

"You do?"

"Yes."

"You might be right, but you might be wrong. I won't know until I give it a try."

After breakfast he dug through storage boxes in the garage, where he brought out an old but usable hot plate and some cooking and eating utensils. He then removed from the linen closet a set of sheets, a pillow case and his old thick olive-drab Army blanket. He returned to the garage and found other items, including the small bedside table with the shaky leg he'd been intending to fix for months. By the time he left for the bar at 2:30 the back seat and floor of the car were covered with his findings, including about half-a-dozen of Sheila's old mysteries.

Sheila, observing, waited to be angry. She wasn't.

A few years ago he'd developed a fever. Though his temperature reached 102, he wouldn't sit still, let alone lie down. He rambled on about one thing and another. Sheila warned him to go to bed. He ignored her. He busied himself in ways he never did when his temperature was right. He fixed the latches on the kitchen cabinet and talked about buying a dog. He remembered funny things that had happened early in their marriage, episodes that she herself and forgotten. After several hours he passed out. She called Doctor Ferris, who came to the house, brought him to, shot him with antibiotics and ordered him to bed.

Now as, day after day, he dug up new materials for The Gypsy's apartment, he behaved as he had when he was suffering from the fever. He was giving Sheila almost no attention. Having felt no anger, Sheila waited to feel jealousy. There was none. What's there to be jealous about? she finally asked herself.

"How's the waitress working out?"

"Perfect," he said.

He started calling her just plain "Gypsy." He left for work earlier than he once had and returned later.

"Gypsy finally went and got the rest of her clothes," he said one day. He explained that he'd told her to sneak into her old boy friend's apartment when he was at work (bagging groceries at Safeway) and snatch them. He lent her his car. He said, "She did it just like I told her and came away with everything."

Another time he reported an increase in customers ("She's really bringing 'em in."), less work for himself ("When there aren't many people at the tables, she comes back and washes glasses and slices up lemons.") and an improvement in the appearance of the place ("She hung red pull-back curtains over the windows.").

Recently he told Sheila that one of these days she should drop in and meet her.

Though she had no interest in meeting Gypsy, she began to feel grateful to her. Joe was avoiding the issues that had heated their marriage for years: Francis, money, late-night drinking. In fact, he'd abstained from whiskey and was now drinking only beer.

"What do you say?"

"I'll get around to meeting her sooner or later." Best, she thought, to leave well enough alone.

Which she was able to do until this morning.

"It's like this," he said, and, with hands dancing nervously over his second cup of coffee, he outlined another plan, lengthily and with many digressions. ("See. The longer I'm down at the bar, the more I stay open, the more income I can bring in. That's just common sense.") He and Gypsy had realized there was a good breakfast and lunch clientele around the neighborhood and therefore thought it would be a good idea to open at seven every morning and stay open until the regular two a.m. closing time. ("We can turn that place into a real gold mine.") He'd had Cliff Waterman, the carpenter, come in and estimate the cost of dividing the upstairs room into two apartments. ("Later I can rent them both out. Right now I can stay in the second one when I have to get up early the next day.") Gypsy, of course, would use the other apartment. They'd share the small bathroom at the middle of the top floor.

Sheila followed a fly passing between them, watched it land on the window in the tiny patio set in the center of their small house, watched it cling there.

Joe nervously clasped his fingers together and pulled his hands back, making the knuckles crack. "Francis is going to end up costing us plenty," he said. "I hope you're not against me bringing in more money to help pay bills."

She found the remark irrelevant and ignored it. Finally she said, "I think you ought to be sleeping here, not there."

"I will be," he said quickly. "From the time we close on Saturday until we open on Tuesday morning."

"It won't do," she said. "Make your choice."

His lips tightened as if his coffee suddenly tasted bitter. He stood and lumbered around the table, stopping beside her chair. "Suppose I told you I already decided."

"It wouldn't surprise me."

"And . . . ?"

"If you sleep there part of the week, please plan to sleep there all the time."

"Are you trying to kick me out?"

She shook her head. It wasn't an answer but a recognition. He'd come back when he wanted, force himself into the house the way he had so often forced himself into her. She too had choices, felt she did, but just then couldn't tell what they were. Even if she'd been able to, she might not have been able to speak or make them.

"Answer me!"

"I don't know."

"Don't know," he repeated, backing into the kitchen, where he slapped his hand against the broom closet door. "Well, I'm going to do what's best . . . for everyone! I'm going to stay there during the week and run my business the way I want to! I'll come back when I want to come back! Maybe I'll never come back!"

He shuffled to their bedroom and opened the closet door. She heard the clicking of hangers. She heard his large suitcase bounce onto the floor. *I don't care*, she thought.

"Where are my other work shoes?"

She opens the door just a crack, sees three clusters of women near the lectern. Lydia, her back to the girls' bathroom, is addressing those in the nearest cluster. Sheila steps out, lowers her head and moves quickly toward the exit door across from the bathroom.

"There she is!" It's Lydia, who must have turned.

Sheila, pretending not to hear, doesn't stop.

"Sheil*ah*!"

Prodded by the eyes she imagines on her, she quickens her step. When she reaches the exit door she doesn't stop but turns the handle, simultaneously twisting and pushing the door open. She rushes up the small set of stairs, presses her hands against the steel horizontal bar on the door at the top and breaks out onto the sidewalk, where she pauses, sucking in the cold misty air, so deeply she can feel it biting at her lungs. After a few seconds she turns, heads woozily toward Kirkham Street, which leads down the hill toward her house.

After Father Gerald O'Brien was relieved of his duties as an assistant at Agnus Dei ten years ago because of public drunkenness, she called him "an unfortunate soul." When Francis in the third grade complained that Sister Immaculata frequently struck children on the head with her clapper, she said, "She probably did it for your own good." She now searches for an excuse for what happened at the back door of the priest's house. She replays the incident in greater detail: the jolting shove, the mother's stumble, the priest's uneasy backward look.

There's no excuse, she thinks.

The fog, instead of rising and dissipating as it usually does in the afternoon, has thickened and descended. It's long wispy fingers undulate over houses and cars and shrubs. A figure walking only half-a-block away appears to be a shadow. In weather like this she's always felt adventurous. When she walked home from grade school in such a fog, she pretended she was lost. Remembering this, she pretends again. *I don't know where I am,* she tells herself. She laughs, feeling some of the old giddiness.

Has she crossed Forty-first?

She doesn't remember.

She gazes at the houses on the far side of Kirkham. They tell her nothing. They could be houses in another part of the city. Or in another city. *I'm lost,* she thinks, almost grateful. By the time she passes Forty-third, her own street, she's lost track of where she is.

She wonders if she should press the game further, say, *I don't know who I am,* until she doesn't? Then say, *I don't know what I am,* until she doesn't?

She told her father about the game, and he said, "You mustn't play it. It's dangerous. You could lose your mind." Then she saw a crazy woman making barking sounds on Market Street and supposed she'd gotten that way because she'd played the game. The sight stopped her, until now.

Released from place, she feels herself being released from time. She remembers the picture that hung above her headboard when she was growing up. In it a white dove, wings extended, hovers over a throng of people. From the wings golden rays descend. The people stand in near-darkness with their hands raised in supplication. The faces are indistinguishable. For years she wondered why the light didn't reach the people. Finally she figured out that the light couldn't reach them until the world came to an end, for that's when The Holy Spirit would descend to earth. She imagined the voice of The Holy Spirit, a low croon, not a bellowing baritone.

And what would he say?

Part-way between Forty-fourth and Forty-fifth she's brought back to the present by the sight of the red tarpaper back of The Sea and Surf building, visible beyond the vacant lot on Kirkham. She finds it as dreary looking as the bar itself. Joe took her inside just after he made the down-payment. The place was terribly dark, even with the lights on, and she detected a urine-smell. He discovered something wrong with the old cash register and started to work on it. Sheila, feeling uncomfortable, went to the back for air, stood in the yard she's now staring at.

She notices something that wasn't there the first time, a wooden stairway leading to a door on the top or second floor. When Joe bought the bar, that door hung in the air. He's put in a stairway. *For her.* Turning, about to go on, she sees movement beneath the stairs. She steps back, behind the nearest house, and watches.

A woman in loose faded blue jeans, bent over, is backing out of the lower doorway, pulling a brown plastic garbage bag, swollen full. When she rises Sheila sees that she's wearing a dark blue sweatshirt, also faded, with red letters that spell WILDCATS across the back. *Francis' jersey,* she thinks, her heart flip-flopping. Why has Joe given her *that?* Francis would surely have used it again, when he cleaned his car or went fishing. No matter. *It's his, not hers.* She wants to rush across the vacant lot, into the Sea and Surf yard and claim the over-shirt. *What else had he taken that I don't know about?* She watches "The Gypsy" drag the bag to the metal trash container at one side of the building. She feels anger but not for the woman she watches. In fact it's pity that rises as the other bends her knees and puts all her weight under the bag to raise it. When she releases it and pulls away from the container, Sheila sees that her light brown hair has begun to free itself from the barrette at the back. Her movements to the door seem more those of a girl, not a woman.

Sheila stands too far away to see that face, is grateful for the distance. In the doorway the woman stops and turns as if she's sensed she's being watched. For a moment her eyes meet Sheila's. But then, abruptly, she turns and goes into the bar.

There was a cold road on a hill somewhere, and Joe had stopped the Pontiac because Francis was sick. It's coming back to her in vivid bits. The road was the winding road that circled not a hill but Mount Tamalpais. They were on their way to Stinson Beach, where there was to be a picnic of some sort. The Fourth of July. That was the occasion, and Tim Meehan, their neighbor, had given them a last-minute invitation. He was a warehouseman at C. A. Swanson and Company, and the picnic was being thrown by the C.I.O. local he belonged to. Sheila was in the back seat with Mary, Tim's wife, and the children, Francis and the Meehan girl, who was Francis' age, seven, but whose name she can't now remember. The men had drinks from Joe's Early Times bottle while they waited in the Meehan living room for Sheila and Mary to re-arrange the picnic basket. Joe was driving, and he'd been taking the curves too fast.

"Slow down, can't you?" she said.

He didn't. There was a hard edge on him, as there often was when he had to wait between drinks. He turned his head sharply and muttered something she couldn't hear. He took the next turn more quickly than he had the one before. Mary, beside her, shrugged, as if to say, "What can you do with them when they're like that?"

Francis, after they'd started up the mountain, stuck his head out the back-door window on the passenger side, inspiring the Meehan girl—Anita was her name, Sheila now remembers—to stick hers out on the other side, behind Joe. After three or four turns Francis pulled his head in and said, "I don't feel very good." Until he was four-years-old, he'd suffered from car-sickness. There had been no signs of it lately. But he until now hadn't been on a winding road going at a rollercoaster speed. "It's better for you to keep your head out the window," Sheila said. He stood and put his head out, but within a couple of minutes he was squatting on the floor at her feet.

"I think Francis is getting sick," she said.

"We're late!" Joe snapped back. "We'd have been there by now if you'd gotten things ready sooner."

The invitation to the picnic had come late that very morning. She seemed to have done ten things at once: make potato salad, take a shower, make a list of things like napkins to be picked up on the way out of town, etc. And what had he done besides take the car to Kelly's Gas Station and buy a bottle of whiskey? When it was nearly time to go, she heard on the radio that the weather was drizzly all along the coast and that the temperature wouldn't rise above fifty. She decided to go into the attic and where Francis' winter clothes were stored and get him galoshes. By then, Joe was in the car in the driveway, tooting the horn.

"Look at Anita there behind me," he now said tauntingly. "She's happy as a lark and not a thing wrong with her stomach." He turned his head and said over his shoulder, "Isn't that right, honey?"

"Yes," she said forcefully. She wore a shiny yellow raincoat. It swished when she turned and gave Francis a superior look.

Francis' head was down.

Sheila bent low and tilted it gently upward.

His pallor was gray. His mouth was slightly open and watering.

"Pull over, Joe," she said evenly.

He didn't answer.

Tim Meehan made a groaning sound.

She turned to Mary, feeling the need for some sort of support.

Mary shrugged at her.

"Up," she said, raising Francis as steadily as she could.

He hung in her arms.

There was another sharp turn coming up.

"Up!" She raised him fully to the open window, held him by placing the palm of her hand against his bottom. He was dead weight against it.

Joe took the turn, as swiftly as he'd taken the last. "It's all downhill from here," he said. She felt the car level off. When it started downward Francis let go.

"Jesus Christ!" Joe shouted.

Tim Meehan leaned as far forward as he could.

Sheila, at the front edge of her seat, did her best to hold Francis' head out the window, but what he was offering came in long steady yellowish streams and some of it fell inside the car. Anita started crying. Francis slipped from Sheila's grip and fell back. He held the edges of the window and, with Sheila pushing, made an effort to help himself back up. Before his chin made it over the top of the window he let go again. Much of what he spilled fell into the window slot. Joe, turning, saw what was happening. "Son-of-a-bitch!" Anita sank, sobbing, into her mother's lap. Joe eased the car into an opening under a mariposa tree, snapped on the hand-brake and flung open his door.

Yes, he was different before that afternoon! Yes, he was! He was cautious around Joe but would speak his needs. Ever so cautiously, ever so evenly, because that was his way. Ever so rarely too. How well, before that, he'd handled Joe! Isn't that the saddest thing?, she now thinks. A child having to handle a grown man. *Sad or not sad, he did it in his own little ways, like easing up behind him and taking his hand when he became cold and remote. And when Joe was angry at Sheila, very angry, Francis would stand beside her and squeeze her clothes where Joe could see his hand, sometimes even squeeze her skin, and stay very close, like a warning or a light or some kind of protective icon* . . . Oh, she doesn't want to go on remembering these things! But they have come to her, have made her their captive.

"Out!" he shouted. But he didn't wait. He thrust his hands into the car and pulled the boy through the window, tossing him onto the damp orange patch of clay where he'd parked.

"Joe!" she said, pressing the door handle.

He turned, leaned toward the open window, caught her face in the palm of his hand, shoved her back onto the seat. Sheila, pulling herself back up, saw Francis on all-fours. He raised a hand and looked at it. She too saw the blood. A stone had cut into the heel of the hand. Joe picked the boy up by the seat of his pants and his shirt collar. He took him over to a small gutter-like rivulet at the edge of the parking area and held him out and shook him. "Get rid of the rest of it here!" he said. "Go on! go on!"

"He can't!" She'd freed herself from the car and, in a couple of leaps, came up behind Joe and pulled him around. In nearly the same movement, she reached down and tore Francis from his hands. "Hey!" He made a weak effort to grab her but she stepped deftly back, turning at the same time, covering Francis with her body. She looked down. The boy was throwing up dry now. She guided him to a tree stump at the back end of the area. She sat down, and he knelt beside her, and she turned her knees and he lay his head over them and delivered the last of his sickness into the rivulet.

"Look at this!"

She turned.

Joe was at the back passenger-side window gazing down. "That smell's going to be in there for weeks!"

She saw Tim, turned around in the front seat, looking at the window and shaking his head.

She saw Mary and Anita at the back window, staring at her and Francis. Open-mouthed, open-eyed, they reminded her of faces at a horror movie.

"Get in the god damned car!" said Joe, turning.
Francis' head moved against her knees.
And why would he want to go?
She remembers Joe coming up to them, standing only inches away. He didn't touch her or make an effort to touch Francis. He looked at them. "Jesus," he said, "what am I doing?"
He was remorseful for days afterwards, but a barrier had gone up between him and them and never, she now realizes, went away.
"Go without us," she said calmly.
His eyes seemed to tremble. "You . . . get in the car."
"Go without us."
He did.
They walked. They found a stream with spring water. Francis felt better after he had some fresh water. An old couple picked them up and drove them to Mill Valley. She had enough for the Greyhound back to San Francisco and fares for the streetcar.
Francis made no movements toward Joe after that, never even when they all appeared happy. He never look his hand or even sat close to him. He listened to him and showed him school work and told him how the track meets went. There was communication but never closeness. Never.

After crossing Great Highway, she removes her shoes and makes her way unsteadily downward, first over dry sand, then through wet, stopping only when her stockinged feet have sunk into the surf nearly to the ankles. Through the fog she sees a huge breaker rise and crash down, watches it spread into a foamy pancake swishing toward her. She pulls her skirt up and lets out a little cry as the cold water swirls around her calves. Seagulls, twisting in the air nearby, screech as if cheering the action of the breaker. Soon she feels sand being sucked from beneath her feet and must step forward, into a new foothold, to keep herself from toppling.

Wasn't it here that Francis nearly drowned? He was a sophomore in high school. She didn't find out about it until he entered his junior year and was asked to write a composition based on something that had really happened. He wrote about the near-drowning. After the paper had been read and graded, she found it on top of the newspapers she's been saving for the next paper drive. She read it. Yes, she's sure, he went in here, opposite Kirkham Street, he and Harold Collins, and they swam out too far, became caught in an undertow and were dragged out for about a hundred yards. They spent an hour fighting their way back. She remembers all the details of the struggle—their cries for help, their efforts to float on their backs, their praying, etc.—as if she'd witnessed the incident herself.

She's left her shoes where she slipped them off. Now she turns, wondering which dunes she crossed. *Those just behind me*, she thinks. She isn't sure. And, suppose, even if she finds the dune where the shoes are, the wind has buried them. She feels giddly. *Suppose*, she thinks, and then she laughs. *Suppose and suppose and suppose.* She goes forward again, lurching this time, nearly falling. The cold water has numbed her legs up to her knees, and now creeps icily toward her thighs. She looks down. There's a wet fringe around her skirt. She sees that the movements she made crossing the beach have freed her blouse from her skirt. The breeze is tossing her hair over her face. She brushes it back, then looks up, searching for the source of a high-pitched chirping that has reached her ears through the sounds of wind and surf and screeching gulls. She sees something tiny and dark, thinks at first it's one of those specks in the eye that sometimes float into her gaze. But its movements are less regular than the movements of the specks. It seems to grow larger which means it's getting closer. It stops, hovering, just above her. She makes out a small bird, and it's holding still in the air. No, not quite still. It's sinking little by little toward her, as if it might be wanting to reach her. She extends her hand. It dips to within a few yards. "Oh, God!" she utters. "It's my little sparrow!" Whether it is or isn't hers, it seems to be wanting to reach her. "Here, little birdie. Here. Here." She flattens her hand, palm upward, to make a landing place. The bird caught in a cross-wind, chirps frantically, beating the air with its wings. A huge gray gull with black stripes across the front of its wings, appears from behind the sparrow, banks and then dives. "No!" she cries out. But the gull smacks the sparrow with its bill, making it spin in place like a top. The gull swings upward and turns. "Come closer," she tells the sparrow. But it makes a desperate darting movement toward the ocean. "Not that way!" The gull dives and pecks it sharply. It sinks, wiggling, into the sea, landing twenty or thirty yards from where Sheila's standing. She takes a leaping step toward it. She's swept back by a rush of water but doesn't lose her balance, and in a moment is plunging on. "Birdie?" She can't see it but hears its weak chirp.

Not far away, she thinks, and, with a great surge, leaps toward the sound. Her feet leave the sandy bottom. She takes a couple of strokes, then feels the backwash pulling her into the next rising breaker. She hears the chirping sound again, but now it's weaker, possibly more distant. She's being sucked into the mouth of a breaker. "Help me!" she whispers. The wave, rising, tucks her into itself, then tumbles down on top of her, spinning her rapidly as if she's made of rubber, then dropping her hard onto the wet sand. She lies twisted on her side, for a while unable to move. Struggling upward, her hands and feet partly numb, she sees the sparrow just a foot or so from her, limp, its wings extended. She picks it up, feels warmth through the dampness of its feathers. She presses it to her cheek, uses her fingers to feel for a pulse. There is none. She looks down. The tiny yellow eyes gaze up at her. "Poor bird," she whispers. "Poor bird." She falls back, exhausted. Her hand opens and the body of the bird rolls out, lies on the sand until the next rise of water circles her and, sliding back, catches it and takes it into the sea. She doesn't realize it's been taken. She's lying still, hoping for a surge of energy that will give her the strength to get up.

BOOKS FROM BOTTOM DOG PRESS

OHIO WRITERS SERIES

#1 *Across These States* (journal poems) by Larry Smith $3.50

#2 *36 Spokes: The Bicycle Poems* by Terry Hermsen $3.50

#3 *Better Things to Do* by Milton Jordan & *Lights and Shadows* by Marci Janas (poems) $3.50

#5 *The Family Stories: The Grennans* by Jim Gorman & *The Benoits* by Peter Desy (short stories) $6.95

#4 *Ohio Woman* (novella) by Phillip F. O'Connor $6.95

#6 *"And a Pencil to Write Your Name:" Poems from the Nicaraguan Poetry Workshop* trans. Diane Kendig (poems) $4.95

#7 *Bodies of Water* by George Myers Jr. (poems) $4.95

#8 *Best Ohio Fiction* by Robert Flanagan, Robert Fox, Jack Matthews, and Philip F. O'Connor—Plus—4 winning stories by Younger Ohio Fiction Writers (short stories) $8.95

WILD DOG SERIES

#1 *Mike's Place: Every Monday* by Michael Waldecki & *Raw Sienna* by Ronald E. Kittel (poems) $4.95

*All books are numbered and signed by the authors.
[Include $1.00 for postage & handling]

For a complete catalog, write to:
Bottom Dog Press
c/o Firelands College
Huron, Ohio 44839